About the Author

Nat Burns retired early from a publishing career in Virginia to relocate to the balmy Rio Grande Valley of Texas with her partner Carol. There, surrounded by palm trees and Spanish tile, three cats tolerate their gales of uncontrolled laughter. And Natty continues to write, compulsively, which the cats and Carol endure with scathing forbearance. www.natalieburns.net

This book is for my life song, Carol, who has always *believed*.

Acknowledgments

Many thanks go out to Karin Kallmaker for welcoming me so graciously into the Bella family. And to Katherine V. Forrest: an editor unparalleled. She helped me rethink my dull, aimless words and sharpen them into more effective tools.

I'd also like to thank all the avid Bella readers who make new books possible.

Chapter 1

Several island acquaintances had warned Nina about Hazel Duncan, owner of the rental cottages where Nina would stay while awaiting remodeling on her new home. And, true to their word, Hazel, called Hazy by the locals, *was* an unusual character. In fact, she was the most unusual woman Nina had met in her entire life.

Upon arriving at Channel Haven, a semicircle of bright blue cottages facing into Assateague Channel, Nina found the small rental office deserted. She waited several minutes, tapping her foot impatiently. She vaguely remembered these cottages; had passed them by many times on previous visits to Chincoteague Island, but knew little about them and had never met the owner.

Not thrilled, to begin with, over the prospect of staying in a rental cottage for several weeks, Nina found herself overreacting to the enforced wait. Plus, her stomach was rumbling from hunger, the moist sea air felt clammy on her skin once she was inside the confines of the office, and her back had stiffened from the long drive. She was just not in the mood to be kept waiting. Maybe she *should* have renewed her lease on her old apartment for another year and then sublet it when her island home was ready. Ah well, she thought miserably, at least this way she would be available to consult on the finer points of the remodel.

After tolerating a few more minutes, she angrily left the office, allowing the screen door to slap shut, and strode onto the adjoining dock to lean against the railing. She tried to let the magic of the waves, and the accompanying wind, soothe her as she drank deeply of the raw beauty surrounding her. As it was approaching midday, the heat of the August sun had coaxed the cobalt of the sea and the jade of the marsh into brilliant hues.

Turning her face into the wind, savoring it, she was shocked to open her eyes and see a woman's face no more than twelve inches from hers. A strong metallic fish odor attacked Nina's nostrils and she backed away reflexively from the woman and the stairway on which the woman stood.

The tall blonde, probably an employee of Channel Haven if not the owner, eyed her with annoyance and brushed past, a string of fish dangling from one hand. Nina watched the retreating back, too surprised to move. The woman walked quickly into the office cottage, disappearing from view. Nina came to her senses and raced after her.

"Excuse me, ma'am, are you…" She paused. The rental office was still empty.

"Damn!" She slapped a palm against the doorframe. What type of game was this? A sound penetrated and she realized that the woman was running water in the back somewhere. Aggression warred with timidity. Aggression won and she moved toward the sound.

Again, she found her nose inches from the woman's as the woman almost walked into her from the back room. She pulled back and assessed Nina for a long moment.

"Can I help you, miss?" Her blue eyes were cold and her

voice sarcastic, the accent decidedly British, typical to the island, but it caught Nina off guard. The woman stirred impatiently as Nina groped for words.

"Are you Hazy? I called…you said you had a cottage…"

The woman nodded, and then sighed as she once more roughly pushed past Nina. This time she took a seat at the large metal desk situated just inside the door.

"Name?" she asked impatiently, pen poised over an open notebook filled with lined paper.

Nina crossed to stand before the desk, feeling like a student about to recite. "Christie, Nina Christie."

Her lips felt tight. Why was the woman acting so boorishly? She was not her parent and Nina resented the way this scenario made her feel: like an aggravating child.

She tried to calm herself. Deciding to employ an old trick she had learned in a psychology course while at college, she pressed a forefinger to her lips. The exercise was designed to make an antagonist less threatening. It was simple really, best if you had time enough to run through the whole exercise. If time was short, at least concentrating on the procedure was enough to defuse a potentially bad situation. She'd used it several times in the past and it had always worked. It was an easy process: study the threatening person and break him down into manageable parts, into non-threatening morsels.

The unfriendly woman appeared to be fortyish, not *too* tall, perhaps just under six feet, not too heavy or too thin. She was muscular though and filled out her thigh-length denim cutoffs and faded yellow T-shirt nicely.

Nina began the exercise with Hazy's head. Her hair was light, a blond bleached almost white by the sun. It needed trimming; the sides which may have once been closely cropped now hung more than an inch or so over her ears, giving her a scruffy, small-child air that amused Nina. Her frustration began to fade.

Hazel's face was unusually square for a female and deeply tanned. When she scowled, as she did now because the pen wouldn't write, lines showed at the corners of her eyes and mouth. Nina remembered her eyes as very blue and very cold. Nina, nevertheless, pushed on; they hadn't been *that* cold.

The body appeared well toned and fit and was bronzed pale brown by the sun. Nina watched, entranced, the interplay of arm muscles as the woman shook and then cursed the recalcitrant pen.

Moving her eyes downward, Nina noticed that Hazy's feet were bare, with toes unpolished but well cared for. There, see? Hazy wasn't so big or so bad.

The woman exploded suddenly, pitching the pen forcibly against a far wall, turning Nina's thoughts into a lie.

"Bloody progress," she exclaimed, more to herself than to Nina. "We should have stayed with the quill." Her voice faded as she bent over the desk drawer seeking a replacement.

Nina couldn't help herself. It really was funny. She giggled and slammed her right palm across her lips but it did little good. The tide would not be stemmed.

The woman's head rose and she eyed the new guest in confusion. This set Nina off again until she knew her face was red and tears were spurting from pressed together eyelids. Hazy must think her totally insane.

"I…I'm sorry," she gasped finally. "It's just…"

How could she explain her amusement?

"I'm afraid I'm tired. It was a long drive," she finished lamely.

Hazy had been watching Nina giggle, mouth open and eyes wide. She shut her mouth finally, fumbled out a tooth-scarred pencil from the drawer and bent back to the paper.

"Address?" she said curtly.

Chapter 2

Nina was assigned to cottage number eight, situated near the center of the semicircle of cottages. Nicely furnished, it offered a subdued plaid sofa and pine paneling. The living area rug, a deep beige color, perfectly accented furniture that was in rich brown tones. A handy desk, chair and lamp lined one wall. The large kitchen appeared to be fully equipped. All she had to supply was food. Luckily, she had picked up a few items from roadside stands along the Delmarva Peninsula for lunch and could deal with the hunger caused by a too meager breakfast.

The bedroom was larger than she expected, with a double bed and a small closet. A tall, narrow bureau stood just inside the bedroom doorway and she placed her overnight case and briefcase atop it. She stood her larger suitcase at the foot of the bed. She would worry about unpacking later.

The best thing about her cottage was the huge windows in each room. They provided a wealth of lovely scenery which she took a moment to appreciate. Most importantly, the water of the channel was a mere fifty feet from her door, right behind a ground-level concrete embankment that outlined the wide Channel Haven drive and parking area. Seagulls and other waterfowl would be her constant companions during her stay here, as well as the soft language of the waves and the warm channel breezes.

Walking outside the cottage, she paused next to her car. She should unpack the rest of her things...she really ought to. She should eat something...

It was no use; the water was irresistible. She strolled across the wide drive that passed before the cabins, berating herself for wasting time when she was on deadline. She simply had to have a manuscript and summary back to Martha by the day after tomorrow.

All that was forgotten as she reached the sloping boat ramp that allowed people to load their boats onto partially submerged trailers and transport them from place to place.

Nina couldn't have found a better place to stay. Family friend Emma Loreli's establishment, called Sweeping Pines, though lovely, was situated on the much calmer Little Oyster Bay, which separated mainland Virginia from its nearest island, Chincoteague. The Assateague Channel, the wide band of ocean that separated Chincoteague and the barrier island Assateague, was much livelier, corresponding more with the ocean's heartbeat. The winds seemed stronger as well, scouring cleanliness into everything they touched.

Her shoes flipped from her feet and she waded in heedlessly. The foamy water grasped teasingly at her calves, let go, then grabbed again. She breathed deeply of the spicy breeze, feeling warm contentment steal over her. This was definitely home.

Later, after a simple brunch of fruit salad made from peaches, cantaloupe and strawberries, Nina got right to work.

Although her parents always pushed to take care of her financially, and her grandfather's death had left her well off,

Nina still preferred to work. She actually enjoyed her job. She had always loved to read, even as a small child, so when she had seen an advertisement soliciting readers for a large publishing company while still in college, it had seemed a dream job too good to be true.

Investigating further, she discovered that although the pay was nominal, she would be the first to read some of the newest novels published. In fact, she would have a part in deciding how a pending novel would be promoted. Because she had a degree in psychology, Jennings-Ryder Books had assigned her to the young adult market and she had been asked to create a detailed questionnaire about how certain novel elements would affect age-specific readers. The challenge had been daunting but Nina had leapt upon it with enthusiasm. Now, after completing each preliminary manuscript, she would fill out a detailed psychological profile of the book and note possible outcomes. She had taken the job two years ago and never regretted the decision.

Martha Jennings, the editor she answered to, had become Nina's second mother and personal cheering section. During the past year, Martha had developed a close friendship with Nina's mother as well and often spent weekends at the Alexandria home of Nina's parents.

Nina sat at the desk, the manuscript before her, and slowly read the final two chapters. Then the work really began. Opening her computer, she thoughtfully, carefully, referring often to notes made earlier, completed a five-page detailed synopsis of the book, a sword and sorcery fantasy this time, then typed in several pages about possible reaction to the work and specific points she liked or disliked as she completed the questionnaire.

Free wireless Internet access had been one of the selling points of Channel Haven and Nina logged on, using the information provided on a card next to the lamp. She called up her e-mail account and wrote Martha a long chatty letter, attaching the questionnaire and summaries. Afterward, Nina hesitated a considerable time, gathering courage, and then opened her inbox. She was crushed to see nothing from Rhonda. Her mother had written, however, and Nina was glad to hear gossip from home. Her old home. Several friends had written as well and Nina spent a good while answering everyone, telling each how excited she was about her new island home.

Altogether, it took her four hours and after sealing the annotated manuscript into a mailer, she was shocked to see that it was half past three o'clock. She rose from the desk and stretched. A hot shower was in order. In the bathroom, a tousled, weary-eyed Nina stared back at her from the well-lit mirror.

Thank goodness this book was finished. Rarely had she encountered such trouble getting through a novel. Sword and sorcery was not something she would have chosen for herself but she was sure the fans of this particular author would welcome it. Now she would have several days free until Martha sent another manuscript for her to read and review.

She stripped and stepped into the hot shower, scrubbing tension from her body, and then slipped into a fresh T-shirt and shorts. Few things in life felt better than a hot shower and clean clothes.

As it was still only late afternoon, Nina decided she would take a quick ride around the island. It would be interesting to see what had changed since her last trip here when she and almost the entire island had gathered to say a final goodbye to her grandfather, Captain Tom.

Chapter 3

Leaving Channel Haven, Nina headed left, circling toward the causeway which provided entry onto the island from the mainland, or actually, from the Delmarva Peninsula. This was familiar ground and she always enjoyed the drive alongside the water. Chincoteague Island wasn't very big so only by going deep inland to the biting-fly infested pine thickets could she escape a view of the surrounding water. Although she'd traveled inland extensively, nothing pleased her as much as witnessing the vagaries of ocean where it met the island shore.

To Nina's left, in the green and gray salt marsh, a lone white egret lifted in unexpected flight. She watched the graceful soaring spellbound until an ominous humming alerted her that her Volkswagen had strayed dangerously close to the guardrail. She sighed and returned her attention to the road, her entire being sated by the beauty of crisp white wings against dappled blue sky.

The causeway road sloped downward and memories escaped their dwelling within her heart. How many times had she traveled that string of bridges during the past twenty years? Many times, it was Nina and her mother, her father too busy maintaining his real estate empire to accompany them. But mother and daughter came nevertheless, drawn irresistibly by the call of the ocean tides and the spirit of the islands.

And Grandpapa Tom, of course.

Nina's mother, Freda Burley, had grown up on Chincoteague Island, the lovely narrow ten-mile long island sandwiched between the Delmarva Peninsula and Assateague Island, the barrier island of Virginia and Maryland. She had spent the first eighteen years of her life in the care of her father, Captain Tom Burley, and a mother-hen housekeeper named Anna Cargill. Freda's mother, Emily, died suddenly when Freda was three, from a cerebral hemorrhage brought on by a second pregnancy.

Yet Freda's childhood had been idyllic. The pampered child of a grieving father and in the charge of a devoted housekeeper, she roamed the island freely, known well by the locals and living closely with the nuances of nature. She had, as the old salts said, the sea in her.

When her own daughter was born, Freda and husband Patrick Christie deliberately made their home in nearby Alexandria, Virginia so visits to the island were a common occurrence. And Freda told Nina the island lore, about the ponies, about the ghosts that haunted the islands, and especially about the one in Woods Grove who carried glowing orbs of other spirits as she searched for her own orb. Freda had also told Nina about her own childhood, her reminiscences full of detail and joy.

Nina wasn't sure she had the sea in her—not yet, not having lived on the island full time, but she did realize her own childhood visits to the island were a precious jewel she would always cherish.

And now Chincoteague would be her home.

Nina studied the small island village, somewhat isolated and abused by the harsh salt climate. The red and blue trawlers, their mooring lines trailing like too-long whiskers from dancing boat to dock, reminded Nina of Grandpapa Tom. She saw his long, fine mustache swaying with each exhalation as he told her stories of the ocean, recalling his days as a deckhand on *Little Murphy*, Norfolk, then as captain of his own boat, the *Lady Say* out of Chincoteague.

Seagulls sported above her car, begging with playful cries. Normally Nina would grin at their foolishness but today pangs of sadness tugged at her. The *Lady Say* was gone, sold to an old friend of Tom's, and she would never hear Grandpapa tell another story, or smell his rich pipe tobacco, or feel the almost painful hug from his strong, heavily muscled arms.

Perhaps living in his house would help keep Grandpapa Tom alive in her heart. Perhaps escaping her life in Washington, DC, would help the memory of Rhonda fade from that same heart.

Rhonda. Nina missed her so much. It was sad to realize that she would never again see Rhonda's lean cheeks crease as she laughed at Nina's bookish ways. Never smell the expensive scent she wore, designed especially for her by her father's perfumery, and never again feel her possessive kisses.

Distracted by persistent thoughts of Rhonda, Nina suffered a momentary confusion at the first stoplight she encountered. Did she want to go left or right? This was only her second trip alone to the island and she regretted those oblivious days of gaping at the scenery while her mother or father drove. Her most recent solo trip, to attend Grandpapa Tom's funeral, had passed in a somber fog.

A large truck slowed behind her and habit pulled her car to the right, onto North Main Street. The sight of familiar tourist shops inundated her, narrow storefronts crowded crazily into their brothers, each window loudly touting the goods within. As a child, Nina had wandered through these stores on scuffed flip-flops, access freely granted by proprietors who knew her by name or as Freda's "gull," the island equivalent of girl. The wild colors in the stores had amazed her; still did today. Nothing in life compared to the bright neon of beach colors and she experienced a pleasant thrill of recognition and longing each time she spied them, no matter where she was.

She passed Dean's Fish Fry where Grandpapa Tom had eaten religiously every Wednesday evening, where Nina and her mother always did as well, whenever they were on the island. Once they'd even ventured out into the empty streets during a hurricane watch just to eat at Dean's. And strangely enough, Dean and his wife, Early, had cooked for them and for the two or three other brave souls who had ventured out under leaden skies.

"I'd just as soon die eating Dean's hush puppies and crab legs than at home," her Grandpapa had stated that night, the words accompanied by a hearty laugh.

Nina smiled at the memory and confidently turned right at the next stoplight.

Here, on Church Street, a different, less busy scene met her eyes. Small groups of rental cottages framed the occasional restaurant, and many private homes, all quaint and well maintained, spread out in welcoming harmony. Sporadic human voices carried to her through open windows, highlighting the constant screech of the gulls. The noise of the sea birds had already become barely discernible background noise, she noted; she had to pay attention to hear them now. Smoke from numerous charcoal grills inundated her senses, making her mouth water just from the memories evoked by the scent. She waved to friends and strangers alike as she passed them by.

Salt marsh stretched to her left, rare on this Assateague side of the island, appearing in certain choice inlets only. The ripe smell of low tide took over and it was like a subtle pheromone, engendering peace in her. Chincoteague.

A fresh burst of hot, moist air rushed across her as she coasted the main curve on Church Street and her bicycle, which she hadn't bothered to unload, jiggled in its carrying rack on the back of her car. And suddenly there it was—her new home, left to her by Grandpapa Tom in his handwritten will.

Her gaze roamed across the property, so soothingly familiar and full of memories. She remembered the house well, had investigated every corner of the imposing structure during the first decade of her life. The old picnic table stood sentinel on the sparse, rocky side lawn. Nina saw herself there, eating warm watermelon, a triangle-shaped slice of melon in each hand, pulp and black seeds adorning both cheeks as she chased the gulls that were circling her awaiting a tidbit. To this day, she was grateful to her mother who, though grimacing with irritation, nevertheless accepted Nina's grass- and melon-stained clothing with equanimity.

The large two-story house was Georgian in style, but certainly was a bastardized version, made of white-painted wood siding instead of the customary brick, and painted white. It also possessed a long veranda-type porch across the front, Virginia's gift to the stodgy New England architecture.

It perched on a rocky, convex curve of the island, just off Church Street, like some ancient gray and white great heron, brimming with pride and age as it stared seaward. The backdrop of the much-loved house consisted only of the pale taffy blue of the ocean sky and the darker, congested blue of the choppy channel waters.

As Nina studied the home, aptly named The Border, she thought of all the storms it had weathered throughout its history, clinging there at the very edge of the land. This sturdy quality made the house perfect for her grandfather, who had eked out a tough but good living from the sea. Both he and the house, though battered by the elements, maintained a warm heart that remained unaffected by adversity.

For just a moment, she saw Grandpapa mistily outlined on the porch and quickly blinked. Was it a ghost? Or simply memory become real?

A horn sounding behind her made her realize she had stopped

the car in the middle of the road. She quickly pulled onto the long gravel driveway as the car she'd detained sped away with a disparaging shout from its driver, obviously an out-of-towner.

She rolled the car along the drive and parked in the front beside a long hedge laid out with borders of oyster shell. The large frame house cast a late afternoon shadow across her car.

So this was where she would live from now on. She let the car door fall closed and walked to the corner of the house. Here was the spot. On the rare days when the wind came from the northwest she could step into this spot and the wind would snatch at her trying gleefully to strip away her clothing, her hair and anything she happened to be carrying. Today was such a day.

Eagerly she stepped into the wind careening around the corner of the house, close to gale force due to the juxtaposition of house and channel water. She stood there a full minute allowing the buffeting winds to cleanse her and, in some ways, strip away her old life, preparing her for the new.

Chapter 4

The staccato sound of hammering reached Nina as she entered the house and closed the back door. A pang of new mourning stabbed through her breast. Her mother had prepared her with the news that Grandpapa had commissioned extensive remodeling on his home just before the sudden heart attack had taken his life. The intrusion still took Nina by surprise, however, and she felt unexpected hostility stir. How dare someone change Grandpapa's dear house?

But she was pleasantly taken aback. She had entered the house through the kitchen door and the work must have begun in this room. The refurbishing of the kitchen was almost complete and she sensed her grandfather's strong presence. It was obvious he was the one who had orchestrated the remodeling.

A new range gleamed from across the room but, in typical Tom fashion, it bore gas burners. Her Grandpapa had once told Nina it was because gas could be obtained more quickly after a blow.

She smiled as she ran one forefinger over the range's stainless finish. How he'd hated depending on the mainland for anything. She saw herself in worn denim jeans and T-shirt, her sun-reddened hair in two braids trailing along her back. Grandpapa stood cooking at the old range, a range polished so compulsively that all the metal had worn to a mesmerizing silvery sheen. Nina, a perpetual chatterbox, was asking him about the differences in gas and electric stoves, how they worked, the pros and cons. And as always, he had answered her questions with slow-moving grace and infinite patience. There were some inherent dangers that one needed to be aware of, he'd warned, such as the fact that gas could explode more quickly, but overall gas was the best choice. Electric lines stayed down but if one could get to Baylile's grocery for a bottle of gas, one could have a hot breakfast the day after a storm.

She felt a little better about the changes then. Just as the new kitchen bore the overabundance of natural wood Tom had favored, Nina knew his many kerosene lanterns would still be scattered throughout the house. It made Grandpapa Tom seem closer.

Nina stepped carefully across the glossy wooden floor and peeped into the small bathroom just inside the hall door. The bath still needed work. The old broken tile had been removed and a new particleboard floor begun. The wooden vanity sat in the middle of the room, and the plumbing lines jutting from its back made it look like a wounded animal. She backed away and a sudden whiff of disturbed Sheetrock dust made her sneeze.

The sound of hammering stopped abruptly and a woman appeared in the alcove separating kitchen and living room. She was short and sturdy, with closely cropped dark hair and snapping black eyes. The deep copper of her skin gave her an exotic look, but the wide smile filled with white, straight teeth was all-American.

"Hello there, can I help you?" she asked, eyes examining

Nina curiously.

"I'm Nina Christie." She waited expectantly but the carpenter seemed puzzled so she continued, "Captain Tom's granddaughter?"

"Oh, yes," she said, hitting her forehead with the heel of her palm. "I'm sorry. You're the one who called earlier. I had no idea you were so young."

Nina raised an eyebrow, amused. She did look younger than her twenty-four years. "I sound old, do I?"

"Oh, no," she replied, laughing. "I didn't mean that. You're just not what I expected."

"Well, what did you expect? Blue hair and diamonds and carefully powdered wrinkles?"

The woman started to say something, then apparently changed her mind.

"Well, yes," she admitted sheepishly. "Either that, or toothy, skinny, with a penchant for expensive fashion."

"To tell the truth, blue hair and diamonds is a good description of my mother. She was the one who called while I was en route," Nina said with an impish grin.

The woman's eyes traveled over her and Nina waited patiently for the woman to finish her inspection. Nina was small in stature, not much over five feet, and it was a pleasant change to be on eye level with someone. She couldn't place the carpenter with any of the island families so figured she must be an import or perhaps a third generation islander. She abandoned her speculation; she was just too overwhelmed to wonder too deeply about the issue today.

"The kitchen looks wonderful, Miss... Sheridan, is it? You did a really good job on it."

"It's Amanda but call me Mander, everyone does, and thanks." She moved into the living room, gesturing for Nina to follow. "It wasn't as bad as I expected. The pipes were still in good shape so we didn't replace them, just added new stuff. You've got a good water system here. Whoever built this house sure knew what they were doing."

Nina gasped as she entered the living area—the ocean seemed to leap into the room. Then she realized she was seeing it through windows and everything shifted back into proper perspective. One entire wall of the living room, the one on the channel side, had been newly constructed of wooden beams and large panes of glass. This gave the impression of actually being out on the ocean. It was an amazing effect.

Eagerly she crossed to the windows, trying to absorb the beauty that seemed to expand the room.

"When did he do this?" she breathed, never taking her eyes from the swelling, slate-colored waves.

Mander moved to stand beside her, appreciating the view along with Nina. "He started it in the early spring. He said all this beauty shouldn't go to waste."

"I remember two smaller windows here. That was nice enough but this, this is incredible. Did you do the work?"

It wasn't really the ocean, she realized, not the whole ocean, only Assateague Channel. It looked so big from this vantage point. She could see a section of Assateague Island in the distance, a blur of green against the horizon. Seagulls circled widely over the swaying waves.

"Yes, I had a lot of help though. My crew helped me set the panes. Captain Tom was usually around too, and he was a big help."

"I sure do miss him," Nina murmured wistfully.

Realizing she was exposing too much of herself, she drew her eyes from the beauty beyond the glass and became briskly businesslike. "So, when do you think I can move in?"

Mander adopted a similarly brisk manner. "Well, give us two more weeks. I plan to use some local workers to help with the painting while I finish the structural changes."

She swung the hammer she held from hand to hand. "What do you think of the way we covered up the demolition of the right wing?"

Nina frowned, trying to coax information from memory. What exactly was she talking about? "What demolition?"

Mander glanced at her, surprised, "Oh, you didn't know? Your grandfather instructed me to knock off the right wing, the one on the water side."

She strode to the wooden door to the left of the wall of windows. "Come out here, I'll show you what I'm talking about."

Full of curiosity, Nina followed. The door opened onto a brand-new wooden deck with a waist-high railing all the way around. Going out to the far edge, Nina looked down at the waves below her feet. An oyster had already attached itself to one of the pilings and salt marks had begun surrounding the two pilings that were visible. She continued to stare down, losing herself in the sway of the water.

A loud whistle finally drew her attention back to Mander. She stood next to the house, merrily watching her. Flustered, Nina walked over, murmuring apologies.

"See here?" she said, pointing to eaves that had obviously been extended, but with true craftsmanship. "We knocked it loose right here and brought the roof out just a little to cover it up. What do you think?"

"I like it," she replied. "It looks nice—like it was built that way—but why did you take Grandpapa's bedroom off?"

Nina couldn't believe she hadn't noticed the change when driving up but realized her approach had been from the opposite direction.

Mander shook her head, a smile of disbelief on her lips. "Because it was falling into the channel. The Captain said you could hear it during the night, groaning as it fell a little further into the water. I measured it when he told me about it. The whole wing was six inches lower than the rest of the house. If I hadn't gotten it off, the stress would have eventually done major damage to the house proper."

Nina laughed suddenly, the sound like small bells in a gentle wind. "Oh no, that's what he was talking about. I should have known."

"What?" Mander was smiling at her.

"The last few conversations we had, he told me that the house and the ocean were talking and would soon be dating." She lifted her eyebrows in mock bewilderment. "He laughed and wouldn't explain when I queried him on it so I just figured he was on the way to senility."

"So now you know," Mander said. "He wasn't so far off."

She nodded toward the boards they were standing on. "I built this deck instead of allowing that destructive relationship to develop. A good thing, I'm thinking. Hey, do you have a boat?"

Her sudden change of subject threw Nina off balance. "What? No, no boat."

"Okay. If you decide to get one though, we can make a dock out of the outer side of this decking."

She pointed to where Nina had been standing a moment ago. "I can open up a section there and build you a ramp going down so you can moor up. Just let me know if you want it done, okay? Tom never had a boat on the sea side, only on the bay, so he didn't need it. By the way, where are you staying until the house is finished?" she asked as they went inside.

The scent of the paint and plaster after the freshness of the sea breeze was giving Nina a headache. "A place called Channel Haven. Have you heard of it?"

Mander gave a great snort of laughter. "Hell yes, everyone's heard of the Haven. It's Hazy Duncan's place."

"Yes, she's quite the character," Nina said as Mander ushered her into the kitchen.

"What do you mean? What has she done now?" Mander asked, laughing anew.

"I just don't know how she stays in business. Doesn't her gruffness put everyone off?"

Mander shrugged. "She has good days and bad. Her better half, Mama New, does most of the tourist trade, with Hazy just doing the boats and upkeep mainly. How did you happen to stay there?"

Nina's heart leapt just a bit. She had sensed Hazy's sexual orientation but certainly didn't feel any type of kinship with her.

"I didn't really remember the place from previous visits here but it was recommended by Mrs. Loreli, a friend of Grandpapa Tom's," Nina explained. "I'd originally wanted to stay in one of Mrs. Loreli's cottages over at Sweeping Pines but she'd already rented them all out for the season and won't have one available till later in the week."

"Oh, heck, I know Emma," the carpenter said. "The Pines stays booked a lot. I just hope you'll do okay at Hazy's."

"Why do you say that?" Nina asked studying Mander for clues.

"You'll see. Just remember one thing. Don't accept anything about her at face value. She is definitely not what she seems."

"What do you mean by that? I don't understand."

With typical island reticence, Mander would tell her no more, only pressed her lips together and shook her head, eyes twinkling gleefully.

"Well." Nina had to smile, Mander's amusement was infectious. "Can you at least tell me where the place is from here? I'm afraid I don't remember what road the cottages are on and I've gotten turned around. I had the address and directions in my notebook but left it at the cottage."

"Don't worry about it, you know you can only get so lost on 'Teague. All you need to do to get there is follow this road out." She pointed to her left. "Channel Haven is on the left, right before you get to Memorial Park. There's a sign up so it's hard to miss. Another way you can spot it is by the color. All Hazy's cottages are painted a weird blue color, as I guess you saw. It's pretty, but kind of shocking."

Mander was moving to the kitchen door, maneuvering Nina along with her. "Well, I'm off to dinner. My crew's already gone for the day. Would you care to grab a bite with me? I know this place that serves scallops that'll melt in your mouth." She pulled the door closed once they were outside, shutting it possessively.

"No, thanks anyway. I'd better get back to Channel Haven before they decide I've wandered back to the mainland. It was a long drive in today so I think I'll turn in early." Nina didn't bother telling Mander that she knew the restaurant well and had eaten there often.

Mander retrieved a battered red bicycle from the side of the house and swung one tan, shorts-clad leg across it. "Okay, I'll take a rain check. Come out early tomorrow if you can. I need you to tell me how you want the shelves in the pantry laid out." She moved down the drive, bike tires crunching in the shells. "I'll see you then." She waved as she pushed off.

Suddenly it struck Nina that she would be living full-time in this house in just a short while. It finally began to sink in: her Grandpapa Tom had left her his house and this house was on Chincoteague Island, a place she and her family adored. Would she learn to love living here as Grandpapa had? She took a deep breath of the warm, salt-laden air. Maybe she already did.

Chapter 5

A cacophony of sound woke Nina early the next morning, just after dawn. Gull cries swelled in volume, died down, and then swelled again as shouting rang out through the cool morning air.

Nina leapt from her bed and ran to a nearby window willing her sticky eyelids to open.

The large bedroom window faced out over the channel and boat rental docks, and she was amazed to see Hazy running along the lower dock shouting and gesturing frantically toward the water. Her loud, accented voice drifted in to Nina.

"Don't be such a bloody tourist, ye damn fool. If you don't know where the devil you are, come back to the office an' I'll give you a map to take with you."

She paused, arms wide, rounded chest heaving, and then began anew.

"Get AWAY from there, you bloody idiot! Oh my gawd, ye're runnin' up on the…that's *my* boat you're tryin' to destroy!"

Muttering to herself, she stalked, steps echoing, across the boards of the dock and disappeared from view. Several moments later, the sound of an outboard motor reached Nina and Hazy raced by, her small craft spewing up geysers of foam.

Nina realized she was smiling. Alone in her room and she was smiling. Hazy was certainly an entity unto herself. She didn't care a fig how she appeared or what she said.

Nina giggled as she pictured Hazy striding across the boards, shouting at the inexperienced tourist captain. She sobered then, thinking how she'd sure hate to be the recipient of that anger and scorn. She peered out the window again and could barely make out Hazy in the distance. She was standing in her boat gesticulating wildly to a group of people on one of the rental boats. Obviously they'd found a sandbar and had gotten too close, maybe even were hung up.

Nina sighed, trying to wake up. What in the world were they doing out this early in a rental boat anyway?

Knowing she had to get the novel evaluation in the mail as early as possible, she mentally kicked herself for not mailing it the day before.

Nina showered and dressed quickly. She rushed to the small, charming post office on Main Street. It was not yet open at this early hour but fortunately Martha always supplied the correct return postage, priority at that, and Nina was able to drop the package into the outgoing mail slot.

She strolled through the slowly awakening town, enjoying the dawn. She stopped at Bren's Fine Dining which, of course, was already open. Brenda Samm's husband had been a fisherman and after his death, Brenda had discovered old habits die hard, such as cooking a substantial breakfast for her husband and their brood of now fully grown children. So she'd opened a restaurant on the outskirts of the town proper and even at this early hour, especially at this early hour, the small, run-down diner was packed with fishermen and a few of their wives. The locals knew Nina and greeted her with friendly cries of welcome as soon as she stepped inside the door. She called back, and waved, pausing several times on her way through the dining area to answer questions and accept condolences and hugs from several of the regulars. She adroitly hurried through, knowing from experience that if she lingered too long, she'd lose the entire day to reminiscences about Captain Tom and every sea voyage he'd ever taken. As she gained the counter, she could hear the renewed buzz of intense chatter behind her, all of it about her grandfather and his life on the island.

Bren waited behind the counter, smiling at her, dark eyes shining in welcome. Nina settled herself on one of the high leather and chrome barstools and cupped her chin in one hand, elbow on the counter. She regarded Bren, noting that she had gained a little more weight and that it added to her motherly charm. She'd had a recent haircut and her riotous salt-and-pepper curls hugged her round head closely.

"Lor' an' if you ain' a sight for sore eyes," Bren said, her island accent strong. "I see where Tom lef' you ta house?"

Nina nodded. "He did and I'm moving here. Here for good."

Bren set a steaming cup of Earl Grey tea in front of her. "Ta. Neighbors are a goodness." She handed Nina a menu. "Got fresh bread in from Ella. 'Sgot little nutmeats in it this time. You know she's always tryin' the new, don't you."

Nina smiled. "Some of her recipes do get pretty wild but they're always delicious."

Bren nodded, then lifted the coffeepot and moved along the counter offering refills to the half-awake old salts sitting there.

After eating a filling breakfast of nut and cinnamon filled toast, jam and scrambled eggs, Nina walked slowly back to her car and headed to Grandpapa Tom's.

Mander was already at the house working when she got there.

"Boy, you're the early bird, aren't you," Nina said, smiling as she entered the living room, a to-go cup of hot tea warming her hand.

Mander grinned at Nina from her perch atop a sawhorse.

She was sawing a thin strip of framing. "Yeah, just trying to get the job done. Early bird gets the worm, they say."

Voices sounded from other rooms and Nina realized, from the strong smell of fresh paint, that Mander's employees weren't slug-a-beds either.

Nina rubbed her nose as she walked toward the pantry. She saw immediately what Mander meant about the configuration. The odd-shaped space could be laid out in two different ways, two sets of deep shelves or three sets of narrow ones.

"What do you think would work best in here, Mander? The wide or the narrow?" she called out.

Suddenly Mander's form filled the space behind her and she smelled the strong woodsy scent of her. The close proximity made Nina's skin prickle uncomfortably and she was reluctant to turn about and face her in the small confined area.

"It all depends on what you want. Do you buy a lot of large, bulky groceries or a lot of cans?"

She twisted around and stared disbelievingly at the carpenter. "What? How do I know what I'm going to buy?"

Mander looked calm, reasonable, but clearly amused. "What do you usually buy? Most people buy pretty much the same from week to week. If you buy a great amount of canned goods, they'd get lost in deep shelves and you'd have to dig around all the time to see what you have. If you buy a lot of bulky items, potatoes, pasta, fresh produce, breads, stuff like that, you'll be needing larger shelves so things won't fall on the floor and you can stack bins in here on the shelves." She paused for a breath, eyes twinkling in an errant shaft of sunlight. "So, which is it?"

Nina stared at the back wall, lost in thought. Who would think of a thing like that? She never would have, not on her own, anyway.

"Bins, I guess. You're good at what you do," she sighed finally. "I never would have considered it."

Mander seemed to glow under Nina's praise but looked downward shyly. "Well, these things are important when you're remodeling or building a house. You need to think ahead so you won't regret it later. Sometimes things can't be changed."

After almost an hour of discussion about various changes in the house, Nina noticed Mander was getting restless.

Thinking she was keeping her from her unsupervised crew members, Nina wrapped up the discussion and quickly bade her goodbye, dropping her empty cup into the waste bin beside the kitchen sink. As she got to the kitchen door, Mander's low voice arrested her.

"Er, Miss Christie...Nina...would you have dinner with me this evening? If you're not too busy?"

She watched Mander's intriguing, dark face, noting the anxious sweetness in her eyes and thought of Rhonda. Then she remembered she no longer had to worry about Rhonda. But she did have to worry about accidentally encouraging Mander when Nina felt no real attraction to her. It had happened to her before with women and, besides, she was just unable to move quickly toward a new relationship. It was too soon. Oh well, she told herself with a mental shrug. An evening out might be fun and she would just make sure Mander knew how she felt as soon, and as gently, as possible.

"Sure, what time do you want me to be ready?"

Mander's face relaxed and she grinned. "Would seven be too early? I thought we could go to Duffy's. It's nothing fancy, just a seafood bar, but the food is fantastic and the company real friendly."

"Good," Nina said with a nod, remembering the rowdy bar. "Sounds fine to me. I'll see you then. I'm in cottage eight." She waved farewell as she walked to her car.

Chapter 6

She arrived back at Channel Haven around five thirty, sunburned and feeling parched after an afternoon wandering the beach at Assateague. After gulping two glasses of cool water, she showered, rubbed lotion on her pink arms and face and carefully dressed. Glancing at her watch, she sighed. It was only a little after six. She still had almost an hour to kill. She stared out the front window.

Chincoteague was such a lovely place, especially this time of day, when the sun was preparing to kiss the earth goodnight. The late afternoon sun slanted across the channel waters, creating sparkle as they moved.

She wished suddenly that she were watching the vision from her own home, with her own possessions surrounding her. She missed her books the most. It was the spare moments of free time, such as this, when she enjoyed browsing through them, seeking the familiar and not so familiar, the words and phrases seeming to always to give her comfort and stability.

She rose from the kitchen chair and fetched her handbag from the bedroom. Opening the change section of her battered leather wallet, she plucked out a carved gold commitment ring that winked at her from the depths. She laid it on the table.

Idly, she twirled the ring around the tip of her index finger, hearing the harsh music it made as it rubbed the Formica tabletop.

How could Rhonda have done that to her? Bad enough she hadn't shown up at the commitment ceremony, humiliating her in front of her family and friends, but then to disappear from the face of the earth without telling Nina anything, well. She had worried about her well-being for days, until a mutual friend had spotted her across town.

Tears rushed to her eyes. Straightening her spine, she let anger fill her. Why had Rhonda even bothered to give her the ring? Surely it was a waste of her family's considerable money. She smiled meanly. Perhaps she should sell the thing.

No, she sighed heavily, she couldn't. Not yet. Rhonda might come back.

Hazy appeared on the dock, interrupting her thoughts. She was closing up the boat rental business for the day, checking the boat lines and tidying up the equipment scattered about the decking. Her movements were precise and efficient. Nina could tell she'd been doing this for many years.

Nina, cupping her hand around her chin, wondered about Hazy's age. Yesterday Nina had thought her in her forties but today, with the wind mussing her pale hair, she seemed much younger. She was unusually fit too, her solid body strong and supple, and this added to her youthful appearance.

But she was certainly a strange one, Nina thought, hard to fathom. She wondered where the woman hailed from, with that strong but precise accent. Old-time islanders often bore such an accent but theirs was harder to understand and it took an experienced ear. Nina thought she could be British. Maybe Australian. What was her history? And why was she so curt with people—almost rude? Was she angry at the whole world?

Mander pulled up outside her cottage.

Over dinner, after the preliminary awkwardness of two strangers coming together, Mander turned out to be a charming conversationalist, amusing Nina with island gossip and history. Nina quickly learned that Mander had *not* grown up on the island but had been a frequent visitor, much like herself. They wondered aloud that they hadn't met previously, especially as they knew many of the same people.

They had driven in Mander's small blue Toyota truck to a tall weathered building nestled between two souvenir shops along North Main Street. The restaurant and bar combination, called Duffy's, proved still to be a popular venue as it was filled with a good number of the island's youth. Mander must have been a regular customer because she was greeted with rowdy cries and whistles as soon as she and Nina entered. In a very short time, they were surrounded by Mander's comrades.

One brawny young fellow, his dark hair cropped very close, moved next to Nina and began asking her questions about her life. She politely answered him and he finally wandered off only to be replaced by another; a thin, gangling girl who tried to impress her with tales of her school exploits.

Nina was flattered by all the attention directed her way but soon found the closeness cloying. Also the mounds of raw and steamed seafood Mander had ordered were pretty only to the true gourmand. By ten that evening, the food became definitely nauseating and Nina decided she'd had enough.

"Mander," she called over the loud music as she motioned her closer. "I'd like to go home now."

"What's that?" Mander asked as she leaned toward her.

"Too much sun today, I'd like to go now," she stated firmly.

Mander nodded her understanding and stood.

Nina was perplexed to notice, out of the corner of her eye, that she leered obscenely to her friends, causing a great shout of laughter and speculative glances directed her way. She felt blood flood her face as she shrugged into her sweater.

Once out in the moist night air, Nina decided not to mention Mander's immature display. After all, no real harm had been done and it would only cause friction that she would rather avoid. She did veto, however, Mander's suggestion of a ride along Beach Road.

"You had fun, didn't you?" Mander asked as they pulled into the Channel Haven drive.

"Sure." Nina smiled. "It's been a long time since I've devoted a whole evening to having fun."

"Well, not a whole evening," Mander teased in a complaining manner.

Nina glanced up and saw desire glinting in the dark eyes. Mander leaned forward and kissed her gently, lips exploring hers in a nervous embrace.

Nina, disconcerted, turned her face away. "I'm sorry," she said gently. "Bad breakup."

Mander nodded and sighed.

Nina opened the door. "Well, goodnight, and thank you."

Mander leaned across the passenger seat and smiled up at her as she stood beside the truck. "I'll see you tomorrow, okay?"

Nina nodded and watched as Mander backed the truck around and rolled away.

Feeling restless and guilty that she hadn't just told Mander there was absolutely no chance of a relationship instead of leading her on, Nina shoved her keys back into the pocket of her jeans and walked toward the boat dock. She realized she needed to be very careful because Mander was working on her house.

Wind, fresh and damp, brushed across her face and swept her hair back to slap against her shoulders. She took a deep breath and pressed her eyes tightly shut for a moment to better experience the salty, clean smells and tastes of the sea.

Rhonda could have been here with her now, she thought sadly. They could have honeymooned here on Chincoteague instead of the ocean cruise they'd planned.

She had found out about Grandpapa Tom's death just two days after Rhonda disappeared. The death would have delayed the honeymoon but the house would have been ready by the time they arrived on the island. If Rhonda had shown up for the ceremony, that is.

Nina nudged the toe of her sneaker against a clump of marsh grass that grew alongside the wooden planks of the dock. Well, Rhonda's leaving had delayed the ceremony indefinitely anyway and here she was, alone again. And planning to stay that way.

Forcing the dismal thoughts away, she strolled along the dock until she reached the wide landing outside the main office. Relaxing into one of the wooden chairs, choosing one sheltered from the force of the ocean wind, she watched the Assateague lighthouse as it hiccupped a muted greeting across the channel.

She was almost asleep when the chink of ice against glass alerted her to someone's presence. Hazy moved slowly across the planks and stood leaning against the railing. She was staring wistfully out across the channel.

As Nina watched, Hazy finished her drink in one big gulp, scruffy hair blowing about her cheeks, then hung her head in a gesture that touched Nina with its apparent sadness.

Nina realized she was seeing this woman in a very vulnerable state and she understood enough about Hazy to know that if she saw Nina observing, she would be very angry. So Nina sat as still as she could, hardly daring to breathe lest Hazy notice her.

After a moment or two, Hazy placed her glass carefully on the wide railing and stripped her T-shirt over her head in one smooth gesture, then, to Nina's astonishment, she also pushed her shorts down and stepped out of them.

Naked, her slim body shadowed, she descended the wooden steps that led to the lower dock and dove head first into the water.

Nina, craning her neck slightly, was able to watch Hazy move with powerful thrusts through the dancing water. She found herself admiring the subtle muscle play in her strong arms and shoulders as her wet skin, lit by moonlight, glistened with each movement.

Hazy went out a long way, farther than Nina would have dared, then turned porpoise-like and began making her way back to the landing.

Nina, feeling very sad again, knew she had to leave, had to make her escape before the other woman arrived, naked and dripping, onto the landing.

But she was reluctant to leave the magic moment; she wanted to stay and explore Hazy. What was it that made her so sad at night alone but so belligerent during the day?

Nina made her way quickly and quietly back to her cottage.

Chapter 7

The next morning Nina woke to a very different sound than the day before. Raising up in bed and pushing her tousled hair back from her forehead, she squinted through the window and saw Hazy outside wading through a seething mass of brown and black.

Peering more closely, she saw that the mass consisted of hundreds of very noisy ducks and geese. Patches of black and white turned out to be clumps of gulls also vying for her attention. The birds carpeted every square inch of Channel Haven drive and even some of the concrete embankment which kept the sea at bay. Hazy carried a bucket in one hand and every now and again she dipped the other into it and scattered feed for the noisy crew.

This morning Hazy had an assistant to help her, a young, red-haired boy of about fourteen years of age and he had taken over her usual duties, helping outfit the fishing boats for customers.

While feeding the sea birds, Hazy politely nodded a greeting to several of the tourists—mostly men—who were lined up for a boat, but kept her attention firmly on the birds, making sure all had a fair share of grain.

"I'll be..." Nina whispered to herself. "She really *enjoys* doing this."

Then one of the white patches moved and rose up and Nina saw it was a tiny girl.

With sun-brightened white-blond hair, and wearing a lacy white dress and shiny pink plastic sandals, she raised her arms, scattering handfuls of grain across the mass of birds. Greedy quacking and honking answered her actions and Hazy laughed out loud.

Nina watched for a long time, noting the mother-daughter closeness between woman and child, until they quit feeding and went into the office, the little girl scampering behind Hazy, scattering ducks, geese and gulls with every skipping step. Who would have thought Hazy was a mother?

After showering and dressing in shorts and T-shirt, Nina walked to the office.

Hazy was just inside the door sitting at the big metal desk. She glanced up when Nina came in and then quickly returned her gaze to the magazine open before her.

"Excuse me for bothering you, Ms. Duncan, but I thought I'd let you know I may be getting some packages here by courier. I left the address with a few correspondents telling them I would be staying for a few weeks and that they could send my mail here." She sank her teeth into her bottom lip. "I hope that's okay. I mean, if you'd sign for them."

"Aye, I don't mind. Be informed, though, that you'll have to check in and pick it up. I'll not be responsible for running around the island looking for you."

Nina's cheeks flushed hot red with anger, but she had no choice but to overlook Hazy's brusqueness, so she thanked her and turned to leave. The sudden entrance of the little girl she had seen earlier barred full departure. She ran past Nina and wrapped her arms about Hazy's neck.

"Okay, where is it? Where is it, Mema? You've had long enough to hide it," she said in a preschool lisp.

"I don't know, ducky," Hazy told her, grinning tenderly. "I suppose you'll just have to find it, won't you?"

"Come, stand up then," the little girl told her, pulling her by the hand into the center of the room. She eyed Hazy a moment, then rapidly dove for her feet.

Hazy was wearing leather sandals and the little girl carefully lifted each foot, removed the sandal and examined it and the foot closely. She frowned and sat back on her haunches, perplexed.

Then she checked the pockets of Hazy's shorts, even running her fingers under the waistband. Hazy giggled when the searching fingers tickled. After feeling under her shirt, the little girl pulled it away from her body and shook it vigorously. Hazy bore all this in stoic silence, an enigmatic smile lighting her features.

"Come down here," the little girl told her imperiously. Hazy grinned wider and squatted down so the child could run tiny fingers around the neck of the shirt. Her knees popped loudly in the still room.

"Hey, no fair ticklin'," she said, finally breaking the silence.

"Open your mouth," the child ordered.

Hazy opened her mouth and said a loud "ahh" as the little girl tilted her head and peered inside.

Putting her hands on her hips, arms akimbo, she stamped one tiny foot in frustration. She studied Hazy closely, as if seeing what she had missed, and then gave a bark of laughter.

Grabbing Hazy with both hands, she smoothed the sides of her head.

Hazy watched calmly, twinkling eyes inches from the child's cherubic face. "Well?" she said finally.

The little girl sighed loudly and continued her exploration.

Hearing the rustle of cellophane, she shrieked gleefully and pulled at Hazy's left ear causing a lollipop to fall into her pudgy hand.

"You're getting too good for me, love," Hazy told her, "I had you thinkin' you weren't going to get a lolly, though, now didn't I?"

The little girl unwrapped the treat and popped it into her Cupid's bow mouth, smiling adorably.

Hazy rose to her feet and arched her back. "You've 'bout got me stumped though, I'm runnin' out of hiding places. Give us a love now, and get on with you."

"I love you, Mema," the child said, hugging Hazy's thigh.

"Ah, get on with you, little bit," she replied, patting the child's bottom and shooing her out the screen door.

Nina, standing just outside the door, watched as Hazy stared after the child with sad eyes. She wondered if they were moist as well. Gone was the coldness of the day before. Hazy turned then and saw that Nina was still there just outside the door watching and the coldness returned like a sudden storm.

"Miss Christie," she muttered with unusual politeness as she left the office, the slam of the screen door echoing as she strode away.

Chapter 8

Mander was finishing up in the pantry when Nina arrived at the house later that morning. New wide shelves gleamed with a hand-rubbed finish.

"They really are lovely," Nina told her as she admired the work.

"Why thank you. Only the finest work for you." She smiled at Nina in a way that made her realize that Mander truly expected more from her than she was willing to give.

"Hey, did you see the bathroom on this floor?" Mander asked with little-girl excitement. "It turned out great." She pushed past Nina and, grabbing her hand, pulled her along with her.

"Oh, yes," Nina agreed as they crowded into the small space. "I love it already."

And she did. It no longer looked like the lair of a wounded beast. Vanity and bath unit were in their proper places and sparkling beige tile gleamed on walls and floor.

"Thank you for all your hard work," she said in admiration.

Mander moved close, too close, and Nina felt annoyance stir. Mander wrapped strong carpenter arms about her waist and pulled her into an embrace. Turning her head, she adroitly avoided a kiss on her mouth and took it instead on the cheek. Mander pulled back. "What's the matter, Nina, I thought you liked women, liked me."

Nina studied her. Even dressed in ragged jean shorts, a tight tank top, scuffed work boots and a backwards baseball cap, Mander was a fetching woman. Most women would leap at a chance to be with her. The chemistry just wasn't there for Nina. She tried tactfully to convey her feelings to Mander.

"I'm sorry, it's not that I don't like you, it's just I don't think I'm attracted to you in that way." She paused, her mind awhirl. "Like I said, I've recently come out of this bad relationship and... can we please keep things a bit more professional?" She was dismayed to hear a pleading note invade her voice.

Mander stepped back a few paces and eyed her warily. "Professional?"

Nina could only return her gaze, forcing her own to be unflinching and unafraid.

Finally, Mander seemed to understand, and she sighed, rubbing her forehead with the heel of her hand. "I guess I was pushing it a bit, seeing as how you're in this new place and your grandfather dying and all. I'm sorry. Can you forgive me?"

Nina smiled. "Sure, Mander, if you can forgive me for being so hard to get along with."

"No problem," she replied with a tremulous smile of her own. "But do you know how gorgeous you are?"

Nina sighed with relief. This was easier ground to deal with. "Well, I think the house is gorgeous. In fact, it looks so good, maybe it needs a new name."

"A new name." Mander frowned. "What kind of name?"

"Oh, you know, something to make it my own, something that makes it even more special than it is now."

"Your grandfather never called it anything other than 'The Border' because of its location on the island," Mander pointed out.

"Yeah, I know," she agreed, chewing her thumbnail, lost in thought. "Maybe I'll call it Channel View because of the new windows or Channel Home because of where the house is."

"They're nice." Mander nodded, mulling it over. "I think I like Channel Home."

"It's okay," Nina answered, "but it sounds an awful lot like Channel Haven."

Mander laughed, but sadly. "That it does. How have you been getting on there, by the way? Hazy treating you right?"

Nina shrugged. "Let's just say I avoid her whenever possible."

"Ah, she's not so bad," Mander said, fiddling with a loose piece of molding on the facing of the bathroom door. "Hazy's had a lot of trouble in her life but she always seems to come out okay."

"What type of trouble?" Nina asked, picturing Hazy in jail, peering through iron bars.

"Well, her parents died in a small prop plane that used to take tourists hopping about the island. Tore her up pretty bad when it crashed."

"Oh, how awful," Nina gasped.

"That's not all." Her voice dropped to a confidential tone. "Years ago she fell in love with this rich gal from one of the better families on the island. Word has it she dumped her. She's been a real bitch ever since, excuse my language."

"That's okay," she mused. "I'd have to agree with you."

"But don't get me wrong," Mander added quickly, "she's a good person if you just remember what's inside."

"That's what you've told me. I'll try to remember that on a daily basis while I'm there," she answered. "Goodness knows, I'll need something to help."

"That bad, huh?"

"I've had a run-in or two with her."

"If she gives you too much trouble, let me know. I've known

her a long time and maybe I can get her to let up on you some. Let her know you're okay."

Nina bristled, feeling annoyed again. "Well, I need to go. I'm going to flake out while I'm not working. Another manuscript will rear its ugly head soon enough."

Mander was following her to the door. "What kind of manuscript? Are you a writer? We never did get to talk about what you do."

"I know. It was really noisy in there after the band started playing. No, I'm not a writer. I read new novels for Jennings-Ryder Books and then critique them. I'm between books now."

"That must be fascinating," Mander said and Nina took a few minutes to tell her how the process worked.

Later, back at Channel Haven, she contemplated her ambivalence about Mander.

All little girls harbored dreams of meeting their Prince Charming and living happily ever after. Nina had been kissed by more pseudo-princes than she cared to remember, and so, long ago, had squelched that fantasy. Turning finally to women was like coming home, a freedom natural to her. Her first woman lover had been a slightly older woman; Nina had been eighteen. Dotty had been a good, kind lover, sharing with Nina all the unique pleasures possible between women.

Her thoughts turned from the pleasure of Dotty to the shame of Rhonda. Rhonda's betrayal had been like sawdust frosting on an ice cream cake.

Mander, now, seemed a perfectly acceptable romantic partner—attractive, charming, good to talk with. But something was lacking. The same things that had been lacking in most of the other girls she had dated after Dotty. There was just no electricity, no spark.

Even the relationship with Rhonda had obviously been lacking something. Sure, with Rhonda's help, she had fooled herself into believing their love would last. But Nina realized now that she had always remained detached somehow, as if looking at the whole scene from someplace far away. Rhonda's every act had been judged by her too-analytical mind, watched and weighed from some other place. Perhaps Rhonda had seen this. Maybe that was why she had bailed out.

Her first love, Dotty, on the other hand, had offered kisses that easily sucked Nina up into them, gentle tornadoes that never let her feet touch ground. No other woman had taken her there yet and she had to admit she was becoming a bit discouraged. Maybe she was destined to be alone forever.

And now Mander. Could she be different than the others? Should she take a chance on her and hope for something to ignite?

She pondered this question long and hard as she sat on the edge of the dock next to the pilings where the rental boats were moored. The ocean lapping about her ankles was mesmerizing, and hours slipped away as she pondered her own life along with the busy crustacean life in the water beneath the planking.

Over to her left, a family—visitors to the island by their Illinois license plates—was gathering around the dock area pointing out the wonders of the sea to one another.

One son, an older teenager, had cast a crab pot into the water and hauled up an enormous horseshoe crab. Nina smiled at the mother's and young daughter's shrieks of horror as they ran to the safety of their cottage.

The two sons and the father laughed noisily. Holding the occupied crab net high, the older son chased his younger sister all the way to the cottage door.

This was all she wanted, Nina thought, a real family. She wanted to have a relationship like the relationship her parents had—two highly individual people coming together on equal ground and deciding to make a life together. Was this too much to ask?

This was all she had asked of Rhonda. And she had really believed this was what Rhonda had wanted as well. They had planned an entire life together. A life perhaps not filled with great passion but with great fondness, certainly.

Feeling defeated and very much alone, Nina strode into her cottage.

The sun set without her as witness; she was sleeping in front of the mindlessly blaring television.

Chapter 9

Early the next day, Nina decided to retreat into her own cocoon until she felt better about her life. She curled up on the sofa with an old favorite paperback, enjoying the island sounds that surrounded her. Then she spied Hazy puttering about the boat rental dock and had a sudden inspiration.

After getting a drink of water to bolster herself and brushing her long hair into obedience, she mustered courage and walked outside.

Approaching the dock, she replayed in her mind what Mander had told her earlier as well as the tender scene she had witnessed between Hazy and her little girl. Could she really be as mean and irascible as she appeared?

Hazy was crouched down into a deep knee bend examining the lower side of one of the small white motorboats kept ready and waiting for customers.

Nina approached cautiously. "Ms. Duncan?"

Hazy turned and looked up at Nina, blue eyes squinting in the harsh mid-morning sun. "Aye?"

"I was wondering if you would mind telling me the rules and regulations of the wildlife preserve."

Her words were spoken rapidly and without much thought. She only knew she felt compelled to talk to this curious woman. "I wanted to take some photographs but find I'm unaware of what I can and cannot do," she finished lamely.

Hazy eyed her a moment, then stood impatiently. "And I look like a tour guide, do I?"

Nina felt her back stiffening. Damn the woman! She was only trying to be friendly.

"No, not really. I just figured that since you're a local, you'd know."

Hazy looked out across the channel, a brisk wind ruffling her white-gold hair. "Let me tell you something, miss. The locals aren't the ones who know the rules the gov'ment sets for the islands. We don't give a fig about them. Our claim on the island is a whole lot more substantial than theirs."

Nina was intrigued that Hazy felt this way. "How do you mean?"

"It's in the blood."

Hazy bent to retrieve a length of rope and, with the power of habit, began to wind it about her elbow and wrist. Impatiently. She shook the circle of rope off her arm when it ran out and then stowed it in the back of one of the boats.

She looked at Nina with indecision, her sun-chapped lips poised as if to speak. Something in Nina's eyes, genuine interest perhaps, must have touched her for she continued. "My father wasn't originally from the islands but came here before I was born. My mother, on the other hand, was the daughter of one of the original fishing families—had lived here the whole of her life."

She paused and brushed windblown debris from the top of a nearby piling. "The pull of the island is so great that, growin' up, the children in my family never learned much about my father's home country, although he did teach us the language so we could understand him when he lost his temper and cursed at us." She laughed lightly.

Nina smiled, enjoying her first glimpse of Hazy's capacity for merriment. Hazy's cold blue eyes had softened remarkably.

"But the point I'm tryin' to make, probably not very well, is once the island's in your blood, whether from birth or a long life lived here, nothing else much matters. It's all about the comin' and goin' of the tide, about when the birds leave for the winterin', and the weight of the ponies' coats telling how harsh the winter weather will be…"

Her voice had gentled into a kind of lilt and Nina found herself mesmerized by the sound of it. Realizing Hazy had paused for a long moment, she responded softly.

"And the full moon on the water, glorious sunrises and sunsets, the rhythm of the light from the lighthouse and the slap of the waves as they come ashore."

Hazy studied her, her gaze appreciative. "You sound almost like a native, Miss Christie."

Nina smiled. "I've visited the islands from time to time when I was growing up. Do you have a large family here?"

Hazy cooled noticeably and Nina could have kicked herself for bringing up what must be a painful subject.

Turning away, Hazy stepped onto one of the boats so she could pull the next one in the row into a straight line. Her voice carried to Nina with the light ocean breeze.

"Lots of brothers, a couple sisters, but there were always a lot of children in our house, even if they weren't from Mother's body. Seems every kid around knew where they could find a warm heart and a kind spirit."

She glanced up at Nina, her eyes sad now, the line of her mouth grim. "My mother was one of those people who actually believed children have something interesting to say. You don't see that much anymore, now do you?"

"No, no you don't," Nina replied hollowly. "And it's a shame too."

She looked up and saw that Hazy had paused in the middle of stepping back onto the dock and was eyeing her with distrust. She wondered what she had said to offend her.

Walking past Nina toward the office Hazy muttered, "Come along and we'll see if we can't find those blasted regulations for you."

Meekly Nina followed, shaking her head in puzzlement. With mysterious, private people like Hazy Duncan, she thought, you really needed to crawl inside their head to try and understand them. Anything else was a waste of time.

Inside the office, Hazy pulled open one of the desk drawers and lifted out a handful of brightly-colored brochures.

"There's this one…" she muttered, leafing through them. "'*Isle of sweet brooks of drinking water - healthy air and soil! Isle of the salty shore and breeze and brine!*'"

"Oh, who's that? Walt Whitman?" Nina asked with interest.

Hazy smiled as she rifled through the brochures. "Yes, it's quoted on one of these brochures. You know Whitman?"

Looking closely at the material Hazy held, Nina answered absently. "Um hmm. What's this one about?"

"Summer programs, you're too late for that one. How about this? It should give you inspiration for your photographs."

She handed Nina a small soft-cover book filled with vibrant full-color photographs of island wildlife.

"Oh, this is lovely. Surely this costs something. Let me pay you for it."

Hazy grinned shyly but with a touch of pride thrown in. "Go on and take it. I have lots of copies because the people who produced it finagled me into helping them. They didn't pay much, so they threw in a box of contributor's copies."

Nina saw her with new eyes. What a complex person she was! "Did you take the photos?"

"What? Me?" She pulled back, as if surprised Nina would ask

that. "I'm afraid I don't know which end of the camera to point, if truth be told. I just wrote some of the information, a friend took the photographs."

Nina loved the way she said "photographs." She put a certain twist of language on it, a special inflection uniquely hers.

"Well, thank you very much."

"Welcome."

Hazy was scowling and muttering as she flipped through the piles of paper, obviously looking for a certain one.

"You're a short-tempered one, aren't you?" Nina told her in a teasing manner.

Hazy's wry look at her was definitely cool, carrying a veiled warning. "I just have little tolerance for foolishness. Ah, here it is. This is the Whitman one." She pulled out a white folded brochure with an island logo featuring seagulls at the top. "This is a good one, tells all about the little critters that are good to photograph. There's also information about the spring and neap tides and what to watch out for when you're hiking about the islands."

Nina took it from her hand, noticing suddenly how a fine down of sun-whitened blond hair covered the woman's tanned forearms.

Hazy seemed to notice her interest and quickly drew back the hand. She plucked out several more brochures. "Here, take these too. This one has the times the preserve is open and other regulations we're supposed to follow."

Silence fell and Nina began to feel awkwardness between them.

"Well, thank you again. I really appreciate all your help. Even though I've been here quite a bit, I still feel like a foreigner sometimes."

"You are," Hazy replied bluntly, "unless you've got the island blood in you."

Nina opened her mouth to tell her that she did have the island blood in her but reconsidered. Perhaps it wasn't a good idea to let this odd woman know too much about her. She had no idea what Hazy would use for ammunition against her the next time her temper flared. The less she knew the better.

Chapter 10

The combination of Hazy yelling and the cries of the gulls woke Nina very early the next morning. Still half asleep, she pulled herself from an uncomfortable position on the sofa, switched off the viciously hissing television, and crawled into her cold bed to promptly fall asleep again.

Sometime later, loud knocking penetrated her deep sleep. A glance at the clock told her it was almost nine thirty. She was worried. Not many people on the island knew her well enough to casually visit. Perhaps it was bad news.

As the knocking continued, she stumbled from the clinging bedclothes and raced to the door.

It was Hazy. She was standing on the stoop outside, impatient and frowning. "Took you long enough," she muttered with ill humor.

Nina straightened her spine. "I was sleeping," she replied indignantly.

Hazy's eyes roved across her from head to toe, her expression scornful. "Aye, I can see that," she said quietly.

Nina realized then that she was half-naked, clad only in a thin T-shirt and bikini panties. She probably looked a mess as well, her hair tangled and her face smudged with sleep. Angry because Hazy was seeing her at less than her best, Nina shot words out like bullets, a bit more forceful than necessary. "What do you want anyway?"

Hazy narrowed her eyes and her lips thinned. "Phone for you. In the office." She turned smoothly and walked away.

Nina felt bad for being so abrupt but decided it was well-deserved payback. Hazy had been short with her plenty of times.

Hurriedly, she pulled on a pair of old jeans and, smoothing her hair, made her way to the office.

"Hi baby," her father hailed her from across the phone line. "How's my best girl?"

It was wonderful to hear her father's voice and unbidden tears sprang up immediately. "Oh Daddy, it's so good to hear from you. How's Mom? How are you?"

His warm chuckle was undiminished by distance. "We're doing okay, honey. I tried your cell but it wasn't available. How are you managing out there all by yourself? Have you visited Emma yet?"

"No, not yet, but I will soon. I've been pretty busy with the house and enjoying the beach. It's fabulous here."

"Good, I'm glad to hear you're having a good time. Is Channel Haven nice?"

Wanting to tell him about Hazy's eccentricities, she paused, knowing he wouldn't understand, might construe that she was unhappy. Maybe later they would look back on it and laugh. After she was settled in. "I'm very comfortable here. Right on the channel too, so it's beautiful," she offered finally.

"And how's the house coming? You want me to come out this weekend and have a look?"

"Oh no, it's fine. Coming along better than expected. Mander, that's the master carpenter working on it, says..."

She broke off as Hazy walked into the office, then continued after she had passed by.

"She says I can probably move in the end of next week. There's still a lot of painting to do and some plumbing in the upstairs bath. Stuff like that."

"Mander, what kind of name is that? One of those strange island monikers?" her father asked.

"It's for Amanda, it's a woman."

"A woman carpenter, leading a crew? Who knew the island would be so progressive?" He laughed.

"Who knew my grandfather would be so progressive?" Nina countered with amusement. "He hired her."

"We sure do miss you being here in town. It'll be hard getting used to you living way out there, so far from us. Be sure and get new cell phone service. One that works in the wilderness, okay?"

Hazy surprised her by handing her a heavy ceramic mug full of hot coffee. Nina nodded her thanks and watched as Hazy took her own cup outside.

"Come on, Daddy, don't be silly. You just live in Alexandria, not Asia. You're not far away at all."

"True, true," he chuckled, "just seems that way."

"Besides," she continued, "it'll give you two a good excuse to take a lot of vacation trips to the ocean. Grandpapa's house still has a lot of rooms so we can all stay right there. Where is Mom, by the way? I need to ask her what color she wants her old room painted."

"Out taking her walk." Nina could hear the grin in his voice. "She'll be mad as a hornet when I tell her I called you while she was out."

Nina sighed and took another sip of the surprisingly good coffee. Hazy had even added sugar and a generous dollop of cream. "You'll never change. Why do you two compete the way you do? I know both of you love me."

"Of course, but that's not why we do it. She gets to take you shopping; I get to call you. She gets to pack up your apartment; I get to send you a book. Simple really."

"Right," she replied with sarcasm. "Hey, did you send me a book?"

Patrick Christie laughed at his daughter's eagerness. "Yes, honey, that new anthology. Science fiction, of course, the one you've been raving about."

"You are so sweet, thank you." She hoped he could tell how much she appreciated his thoughtfulness. He often bestowed solicitous gifts on her and she always felt as though she could never express the depth of her gratitude and love for her handsome, doting father.

"You're welcome, baby. Listen, I'm going to go now, before your mother comes in and catches me red-handed. You call us right away if you have any problems, all right? Promise?"

"Sure, I promise. Everything's going fine though. I am really glad to be moving here."

"I know how much you love it there," he agreed. "That's why Tom left it to you instead of Freda. He knew you'd build a good life there."

A sudden thought occurred to her. "Why are you at home this morning? You're not sick are you?"

"Oh no, please don't start worrying. I hate it when you worry about me. I'm just going in a little late, leaving for work in just a few minutes." His confident voice warmed her. "Love you sweetheart. Be good, now."

"Hey, Daddy." Her voice broke, but she couldn't help asking. "Any word from Rhonda?"

Her father's voice was filled with empathetic pain as he answered. "No, baby, nothing. I'm really sorry…"

"That's okay, Dad, for the best, really. Tell Mom I love her. You too."

Although hating to break the connection, she was relieved to know he was leaving for work. Her powerful father hadn't missed a full day, not counting vacations, from his real estate firm in more than twenty years.

Slowly she replaced the handset and sighed. She did miss them. Even when she'd moved away from home when she was twenty, she had taken an apartment nearby. This was the farthest she'd lived from them and it would be a drastic change, she was sure. But she was a big girl now. It was time she got out on her own.

Chapter 11

Hazy was leaning against the dock railing watching two gulls fight over a large sea worm that one had pulled loose from a hole in the piling. She saw Nina out of the corner of her eye and realized with some surprise that Nina seemed nervous about approaching her; almost didn't. But she did approach and Hazy sighed.

"Thank you for the coffee. It helped wake me up."

Hazy turned her attention Nina's way, her gaze taking in the whole of her. As if self-conscious, Nina crossed her arms over her chest protectively.

"That's all right, ducks," Hazy said, squinting to peer into her large green eyes. "Always a waste, that last little bit in the pot. Glad to use it up."

The tone Hazy had used obviously angered Nina and she stiffened her back. "Right," she muttered. "I'll wash the cup and return it before the end of the day," she said, her tone just as cool.

Head held high, she walked back to her cabin.

Hazy watched the rigid sway of her denim-clad hips and felt regret swamp her. Damn, but she liked the little chit. She had a way about her. Tough little sandpiper, didn't take no guff from anyone and gave as good as she got. She couldn't help but admire her. It was just a shame she had to like her as well.

She took a gulp of her lukewarm coffee and grimaced at the harsh taste. Why had she told the girl she'd gotten the dregs? It was a lie, to start with, and there was no call to be so rough with her.

Ah, but there was. She dropped her head and hunched her shoulders. She mustn't forget CC. *Miss* Claudia Coleman Marsten, CC to her friends, the prized darling of the Chincoteague Marstens. Hazy hadn't realized the ramifications of that at first, of course, or she'd have steered clear. No use butting one's head against a brick wall.

They'd been so alike, she reminisced. Both with a streak of fun in them; do most anything for a laugh. Silliness was what brought them together.

So many years ago yet she still saw it with crystal clarity.

Working as a proofreader for the *Chincoteague Wagoneer*, the small island newspaper, Hazy had thought that journalism might be her field. Fresh out of high school she was an old hand at the job because she'd worked at the paper all through school, gradually advancing from "gofer" to proofreader. Words came easily to her and it was a natural gift to place them on paper in the best way so they could be understood easily. She knew one of the older staff writers was due to retire the following year so Hazy was seriously considering vying for that position. Or the position of whomever, in house, might move up into that slot.

There was a young girl who hung around the office in the evenings, the daughter of one of the owners. She was lovely, small and slim, with blond, silky-shiny hair sleekly cropped off at shoulder length and often pulled back into a short ponytail. Her nose was long, patrician, her mouth small, her white teeth dainty. Her blue eyes were speculative, cool, and could convey unbelievable disdain if she was provoked. Hazy knew; she had watched her for years, fantasizing about the two of them together.

One day, as Hazy was working on the social register, she felt the hair on the back of her neck rise. She turned and saw the girl reading over her shoulder. She smiled sweetly as Hazy caught her with her eyes. Hazy, cherishing her good fortune, returned the smile.

The girl reached out a slim, perfectly-manicured index finger and touched a word on the copy sheet. It was high up on the page, in a paragraph that had, supposedly, already been proofread and corrected. Hazy lifted an eyebrow and bent to read the word: "boby." Confused, she went back several words to put it in context.

Mr. and Mrs. Carlton E. Wooby announce the birth of a boby boy. Oliver Everett Wooby was born at 6:25 a.m. Tuesday. Mother and son are both doing well.

How had she missed it?

Before she could pen in the correction squiggle, the girl leaned forward and sketched in another 'o' next to the word boby.

"Booby Wooby," she said, light dancing in her eyes.

Strangely enough, Hazy left it as it was and it came out that evening as booby boy Wooby. That was an unHazy-like thing to do, just as was the passionate relationship that sprang up between the two of them. Fast, furious, and in the end, destructive.

It began to unravel several months later when Hazy's calls weren't picked up and were never returned. Worried, she'd gone to the high school during her lunch hour. On the second day of watching she saw them, walking arm in arm toward the gym. He was a handsome boy, right enough, but when they moved into an alcove and the kissing started, Hazy had stalked off, unable to watch.

Hazy blamed herself at first, spending days locked in self-loathing and pity. Then she realized that CC was a certain type of girl. There had been several of them at their high school. They experimented, lived for the moment, took what they wanted, whatever made them feel good for a short time, and then moved on when the excitement paled. Hazy wasn't stupid, she knew the type and should have had her guard up.

She'd made a solemn vow when CC had dumped her so cruelly. She'd never be hurt that way again.

And she hadn't, not in almost twenty years. No woman had ever touched her heart. Her conquests had been the wealthy, older tourists or the young, still innocent island girls. The former knew the score; the latter had yet to learn.

She had always been able to mentally criticize each woman, pick her to pieces until there was nothing left to threaten her peace of mind. By that time the relationship was stripped to the bone as well, leaving nothing to nourish it.

Hazy was well aware of this trait in herself and rather enjoyed the irony of it. Who needed a woman trying to edge into her life? She could love them and leave them as easy as anyone. Since CC, she'd never had the desire for anything more than the coolest of relationships.

Until now.

She almost dropped her coffee cup into the channel and had to fumble quickly to catch it.

Now where had that thought hailed from? She looked around the dock scowling. She guessed that the tiny slip of a girl was beginning to get under her skin after all. Walking quickly into the office, she reassured herself. It was okay. Nothing she couldn't handle.

Chapter 12

Nina was feeling even sadder after talking to her father and sparring with Hazy, so she showered and threw on some of her oldest clothing and rode her bike out to Grandpapa Tom's house. Physical exertion was usually effective in banishing the blues and since there was painting to be done at the house, she felt she was a prime candidate for the job.

Parking her bike at the side of the The Border, she whipped a large handkerchief out of her back pocket and tied it carefully over her hair.

Mander was in the large living area nailing a piece of mitered baseboard to the wall near the kitchen door. Workmen stirred and talked softly in adjoining rooms.

"Hey there," she called, upon catching sight of Nina.

"Hi Mander, can you use a little help today? I need to occupy my mind."

Mander looked surprised but answered readily enough.

"Sure, I never turn down an offer of help. What did you have in mind?" She swiped at her forehead with a balled-up cloth.

"I thought I could paint a little. I wield a pretty mean paintbrush, or so I've been told." She smiled impishly, trying to show her they could still be friends.

Mander returned the grin.

"Well, *okay*," she sighed and rubbed her palms together, "let's see what we can do with you. Danny has already started on this room and Ray is in the other. I'll get you to do one of the bedrooms upstairs."

She started for the stairway. "Let me open the paint and stir it around for you."

"Whoa," Nina cried quickly, "get back here. There's no need for you to do all that. I'm perfectly capable. Just go back to what you were doing. I'll call you if I need help."

"Okay." Mander watched her mount the stairs. "The roller and pan are in the bottom of the closet and the paint should be in the center of each room."

Her cheery 'thanks' floated down the staircase as Nina ascended.

She was intrigued by the changes that Mander's crew had made to Grandpapa's home. The walls along the stairway, which had once been pocked with age, had been replaced with new Sheetrock and painted a subdued dove gray. The steps and risers had been sanded and sealed with polyurethane, as had the floorboards of the landing and the long upstairs hallway. The four rooms on this floor had been mostly unused after Freda had moved away. At one time, Tom and Emily had shared the master bedroom, but after her death, Tom had begun sleeping downstairs in a small room off the kitchen. He'd been content with a single cot, a stack of books and a lamp. Freda's room had been at the end of the long upstairs hallway, with Anna, when her husband was away at sea, sleeping in the smaller bedroom next to Freda's. Anna's room was Nina's favorite as it faced east and had a full-on view of the channel. It was colder than the other rooms in the winter, however, and stepping inside, she was glad to see that Mander had installed modern double-walled glass windows and a new heat register.

She and Mander had already discussed the paint colors her grandfather had chosen and she had opted to leave them unchanged. It somehow kept him closer. As she pried open the paint can, she was gratified to see the color he'd chosen for Anna's room, as Nina had always referred to the room she'd used while there, was a lovely robin's egg blue.

Painting her new bedroom was the perfect chore. She could be alone to think about her life and the choices she would need to make. Like how she was going to avoid Mander's advances, for example. What was it about her that was so annoying? She frowned and applied pastel-tinted paint to the south wall.

If only she could pinpoint exactly what bothered her about Mander, maybe it would help. As it was, with her feelings undefined, she felt as if it would be wrong to deny a relationship; it would be like not allowing Mander a chance to prove herself.

Yet she didn't want a relationship, did she? Not like that. She wanted something *real*, permanent and thrilling, something that made her feel loved for all the right reasons. Mander just wasn't *it* and there was nothing she could do to change that, Nina decided.

The afternoon sun was a pale glow when she finished the room. She stood back and admired her handiwork. It was lovely; the pale blue walls were made almost ruddy by the spreading sunset reflecting off the channel water. It'll be lovely to lie in this room when the sun comes up, she thought. She envisioned a lot of white furnishings in this room with maybe an occasional touch of light pink. Her Grandmother Christie's white lace bedspread came to mind. It would look fabulous on a big four-poster bed in this room.

Hands clasped her from behind as she stood musing and a firm body pressed against her from shoulder to knees. Warm lips pressed into the curve of her neck and a sudden startling image of Hazy Duncan filled her mind.

Whipping around she was actually surprised to see Mander.

"Mander," she gasped, her face flushed and heart pounding.

Mander spread her hands and frowned in confusion. "Who'd you think it would be? Lon Chaney? Count Dracula?"

Nina smiled weakly. "No, no, of course not. You just startled me sneaking up like that. You should be ashamed, scaring poor defenseless girls."

Mander indicated the paint roller Nina still held upraised in a threatening stance. "I wouldn't say defenseless."

"Oh, sorry," she said sheepishly as she lowered it.

"I just wanted a little snuggle, that's all." She took Nina in her arms again, kissing her kerchief-covered forehead. "Wanna go grab a bite with me? I'm done for today and you should be too."

Angered by the unwelcome familiarity, especially after their previous discussion, she nevertheless tried to avoid being too harsh. "Yeah, I am done. What do you think?" She pulled away to spread her arms and rotate slowly. "I did a good job, huh?"

Mander squinted and strode over to examine one wall. "Yep, sure did. Couldn't have done better myself. Now, how about dinner. You hungry?"

Nina chewed her bottom lip, raising uncertain eyes to meet Mander's. She felt like such a coward and didn't understand why she couldn't be more forthright. "I don't know, Mander. I'm really not too hungry. My...my stomach's been a little upset today. I think I'd rather go home, take a long, hot shower and pop right into bed."

Mander looked at her dubiously, then finally said quietly, "Yeah, probably too much seafood the other night. It affects a lot of people that way."

Chapter 13

Nina showered for a long time, scrubbing the paint from her body and washing her sweat-dampened hair. The hot water lifted her spirits and, feeling refreshed, she reached to turn off the water.

The cold water knob came off in her hand when she'd turned it about half the way closed.

She sighed wearily and pressed her palm to her cheek. She supposed she'd have to get someone to fix it so it wouldn't run all night.

After drying and pulling on clean jeans and a shirt, she walked across the drive and, to her dismay, found the office closed. A small hand-lettered sign directed after-hours visitors to the back door. Searching around the back of the cottage, Nina finally paused in front of a blue wooden door with flowers planted at each side. The door was on a ninety-degree angle to the dock so she took a minute to take a breath and gain strength from the rocking ocean.

From inside she could hear soft music and, as she listened, the station was changed to one that played lilting flute music. How she hated to bother Hazy and her family this way.

After wiping her suddenly damp palms on denim-covered thighs, she lightly rapped on the wooden door. Immediately the music stopped and she could hear a board creak as someone approached. The door opened.

Hazy was barefoot and clad in a T-shirt and a pair of loose cotton shorts. Her blond hair was tousled and her eyes warmer than Nina had ever seen them, except maybe when she was playing with her little girl.

"Ms. Duncan," began Nina, nervously twisting her hands together. "I'm afraid my shower has broken. The knob came off in my hand and the water is running."

Hazy surprised Nina by grinning openly—it was a real smile, no sarcasm. "Yeah, cottage eight. It's happened before and I told Manny it needed to be changed out. Cold water, eh?"

When Nina nodded, Hazy laughed softly and said, "Hang on a minute then. I'll get the tools."

She paused, clearly wondering whether to invite Nina in. Pushing the wooden door wider, she left the screen door closed, saying, "Step in while you wait if you've a mind to," and disappeared into the back.

Nina's curiosity won out over her timidity and she opened the screen door and stepped inside. And gaped like a toddler seeing snow for the first time.

Shelves, nicely made to fit, covered every inch of wall space and there were freestanding bookcases in those places where wall-hung shelves were impractical. Each shelf was crowded with books, a few shelves here and there displayed driftwood and bare shelving instead but they were very few when compared to the book-filled ones.

Now, who would have thought Hazy would be a reader? Nina shook her head. It had to be her partner.

The rest of the cottage was littered with haphazardly dropped toys, but was basically neat and spartan—a battered but comfortable looking sofa and armchair, a coffee table crafted from driftwood and pine, a lamp, and toward the back, a cramped but tidy kitchen with a small TV on the counter. There was no table, only a bar which was currently littered with Barbie dolls and their wardrobes, and two stools on the living room side. A door at the far end of the living area was closed and Nina reminded herself to move quietly and not wake Hazy's partner and little girl.

At a sudden scratching sound Nina whirled to face the unknown. It was an old fashioned stereo turntable over to her left. Hazy must have only turned down the volume when Nina knocked instead of taking the needle off the album. Now the vinyl album was finished and the needle was scraping against the center paper.

She quickly stepped over a doll and a stuffed horse to place the needle arm back into its holder. Vinyl records? She couldn't help but notice what Hazy had been listening to—flautist James Galway's *Melodies from Japan*. She recoiled a bit in surprise. This could not be the same woman who took a shark bite out of her emotions each time their paths crossed.

"Well, here I am. I'd left them out back by the—" Hazy came in through the kitchen, saw where Nina was standing and broke off abruptly.

"Do you read?" Nina breathed without thinking. Eyes wide with wonder, she studied Hazy. "I can't believe you read."

Hazy scowled. "They do teach it in school, you know, even here on this backwater island."

Nina blushed crimson and fidgeted with the hem of her shirt. "I-I'm sorry. I only meant...a lot of people dislike reading in this TV age. I just assumed you were the majority and didn't care for reading. I wasn't trying to insult you."

Her heartfelt apology seemed to touch Hazy. "'S'okay, ducks. Let's get that water off before the pump gives out." She held open the screen door and ushered Nina through it.

"Who's your favorite author?" Nina asked as they crossed the drive. A sudden wind blew across, spattering them with sea foam.

"Don't really have one," Hazy replied quietly. "I like different things about different writers. Bradbury's poetic style appeals but I like Michener's detail as well. I just read whichever I'm in a mood for. How about you?" She turned to glance at Nina's profile.

"I'm pretty much the same, I suppose, although I can never seem to turn down a Stephen King or a Fredric Brown."

They arrived at her cottage and Hazy actually held the door open for Nina as she entered. "I suppose they're all right if you like seeing the sordid side of things close up. I do particularly remember a Brown story, the one about the giants that invaded and started spraying clouds of stuff. *Insecticide*, was the name, wasn't it?"

Nina frowned as she concentrated. "I believe it was *Pattern*. I remember it but never thought it was one of his better works. I'll have to let you borrow an anthology I have of his good stuff after I move in and my crates arrive from storage."

She bestowed a teasing grin on Hazy. "If you don't already have it, that is. It could be hiding in there and you'd never know it."

Hazy smiled as she moved into the bathroom and called out, "No way. I know each of my books personally."

Nina believed it, for some odd reason. Again she delighted in the way Hazy said the word *personally*. It was enchanting. She leaned one shoulder against the bathroom door facing, wishing she'd thought to pick up her wet washcloth from the floor lest Hazy think her a slob.

She needn't have worried. When her bare foot encountered it, Hazy absently retrieved it and draped it across the metal loop inside the enclosure. She bent to peer closely at the knob, all the while dodging the water flow.

"I think I'll need the pliers," Hazy muttered. Nina dug into the toolbox, her hands clumsy and fumbling.

The special scent of Hazy filled the small bathroom, the smell of sweet ocean foam, spicy and compelling. It suddenly overwhelmed her senses.

It spread over her rapidly. She glanced at Hazy briefly. Did she feel it too? She was waiting for the pliers, head down, her bottom lip caught between her teeth, ignoring the cold water that was dampening the hem of her shorts and her legs.

Nina held the pliers clenched in her hand, reluctant to get close enough to hand them to Hazy.

"Here," she said, the word choking her. She held out the pliers.

And then Hazy looked at her. Nina felt the impact down to her toes. The fire in the woman's bright blue gaze jolted her body into new awareness. Wordlessly, Hazy dropped her gaze and plucked the tool from Nina's nerveless fingers.

The tension in the tiny room continued to swell and Nina felt as though her blood was boiling within her body. Her heart was sluggish; it didn't seem to want the trouble of beating. Afraid she would begin gasping for air, she mumbled an excuse and fled the bathroom.

In the bedroom she sat on the end of the bed and sank her teeth into the fleshy part of her thumb. What had happened in there? One moment they were talking normally, the next... Tension; very different from their normal animosity. She had felt compelled to touch Hazy, had wanted to feel her hair, to feel her skin beneath her palms. She had, God forbid, wanted to wrap her body around that sleek muscled form.

Perhaps she was overreacting. Perhaps it was just the close proximity and the budding feeling of kinship. After all, this was the first time they'd been civil to one another for any length of time.

What about those eyes? They had seared through her. There was a message there, a message of passion waiting. Waiting for her. She held her breath as she relived the passionate jolt she'd felt when Hazy looked at her.

Just outside the bedroom door, Hazy cleared her throat.

Heart leaping, Nina jumped up, trying to pretend nothing had happened. She knew her color had to be high.

"That's that then. The knob I put on doesn't match but don't let it worry you. Old one's stripped finally so I'll just order a new one from Harper's over on the shore. It'll be here in a few days. I'll check back then, all right?"

"Yes," Nina stammered, hazarding a glance at Hazy. "Yes, that'll be great. Thanks for coming out so late to help."

"No sense letting the pump run all night. Wouldn't do anybody any good now, would it?" Hazy's eyes were still warmed by passion but the words chilled.

She moved quickly out the door, letting the screen door slap shut behind her.

Hazy fairly flew across the drive. She dropped the tool-box outside the office and paused to look back at cottage number eight. She could see Nina framed in the bedroom window slowly brushing her long hair. How could one woman be so beautiful and so bloody *sweet*? Beautiful women were always cold, always stuck on themselves, believing they were better than lesser mortals. Hazy didn't sense any of that in Nina. And she loved books, obviously, a passion the majority of women Hazy had dated knew nothing about.

Hazy could have kicked herself. When she had begun to think of Nina naked in the shower, she shouldn't have allowed her thoughts to linger. But the pleasure of the imaginings…Why had she looked at Nina then, exposing herself that way? Stupid! Stupid. She might as well have handed her a knife and exposed her jugular.

She pressed her forehead into the worn blue clapboards of the office wall and groaned. Oh sure, right-o, she had everything under control. She had really thought she could ignore her as she had the others. She was sure of one thing now: she was in deep trouble.

Chapter 14

The next day Nina straightened up the cottage, took a shower, and then pulled on shorts and a T-shirt. She was still feeling homesick after talking with her father and knew that the only remedy for such maudlin thinking was some sort of activity requiring her full attention.

Eagerly she packed a small backpack with a jug of water, insect repellent, sunblock, field glasses, informational pamphlets about the islands, a sack lunch and, especially, her digital Nikon camera with its telephoto lens.

Donning hiking boots and a biking helmet for safety, she slung her pack over her shoulder and fetched her bike from its resting place in the bedroom.

Pedaling fast along the wide bike trail that paralleled Beach Road onto Assateague Island, Nina fully enjoyed the wind in her face, rich with sea and marsh smells. She waved to the guard, a familiar face she couldn't quite place.

As she pulled onto the wide asphalt loop that ran through the wildlife refuge, she realized she probably would have it all to herself because today the road didn't open to vehicles until late afternoon. Delighted, she pedaled on.

Pausing at the first overlook, she walked her bike to the podium-style platform. Pulling the field glasses from her pack and, leaning her elbows on the platform, she gazed out across the marsh. Few animals seemed active in this particular area of the marsh. When only one black skimmer passed her by with a disdainful squawk, she moved on.

Just as she was about to wheel her bike from the pull-off area, a second bike and rider whizzed by at dangerous speed, almost colliding with the front wheel of her bicycle.

Nina watched his retreating back with disgust. "Your black helmet suits you," she called after him. He was certainly a bad guy. Mounting her own bike, she followed at a more leisurely pace.

At the next overlook, she discovered a large lagoon filled with black ducks and Canadian geese. Watching through field glasses, she was pleased to see the ducks play at mating; females following and dipping their heads almost shyly as they proved their interest in this or that male.

The bathing ritual the ducks displayed was also a treat. Nina watched with fascination as one duck dipped its head into the water with a serpentine motion then used the wet head to smooth its back feathers. Plucking and grooming the feathers all along its sleek body was the next motion on the agenda and the duck accomplished this in a small flurry of flying down feathers.

A mother duck following a small brood of half-grown ducklings was winding her way through the tall marsh grass. Holding her head high with pride, she approached the other ducks, soon losing herself, and her adolescent babies, in the dark crowd.

The geese were very noisy as they flocked in a large group that reached all the way across the small pond of water. These large birds didn't seem to be in any kind of social order or pairs, although Nina knew they mated for life. They were lazily milling about, calling with their noisy honking voices.

Rugged Chincoteague wild ponies were grazing off in the distance and every now and again a young white-tailed deer strode into view, warily eyeing the highway that passed within a half mile from its grazing range.

Enchanted, Nina traded the eyepieces of the field glasses for the viewfinder of her camera and started to snap numerous photographs.

Though she never claimed to be a real photographer, Nina's photos were well appreciated by friends and family. She considered them a personal pleasure and derived great satisfaction from isolating a remarkable specimen or scene from background clutter. She seemed to have a natural eye for color and balance.

Sighting one of the tiny Sika deer, really a miniature elk brought to the island by way of the Asian continent, Nina focused and clicked the shutter, excited to locate one of the shy creatures so quickly.

An hour or so later, after a short break for a lunch of peanut butter sandwich, fruit and water, and several more photographs, Nina rode her bike all the way around the wildlife loop and back onto the main road heading south.

Soon she came to the highway that traveled past the beach parking areas. Following it, she spied the wooden walkway that led into the Tom's Cove Nature Trail, something she had wanted to explore for a long time.

Parking her bike in the weeds alongside the road, she hefted her pack and set off along the wooden plank path through the marsh. Fiddler crabs scurried frantically as her footsteps sounded on the boards.

She remembered the time her grandfather had teased her with a handful of the frantic little crustaceans, finally dropping them right in her lap, causing her to shriek and run away, only to be pulled back to them by avid curiosity. A smile touched her features as she relished the memory.

After walking for some time, she paused for several gulps of lukewarm water and to read the informational plaque placed by the forest service. It told how the two-mile hook of land encircling Tom's Cove had been growing larger over the years, gradually providing more and more land to the southern tip of Assateague Island.

Looking out over the land and sea junction with her field glasses, she noticed blue crabs and horseshoe crabs sprawled across the sand. Seagulls and other buff-colored birds were feeding on some of them.

Moving along, Nina left the walkway and took a number of photographs in the marsh, mostly close-ups of the elusive fiddler crabs which required enormous patience and perseverance.

Finally, hours later, exhausted and dirty, she made her way back to the main road near the beach.

As she neared the road she spotted a great mass of brown. Squinting her eyes into narrow slits, she peered toward the trail entrance, noting movement in the mass. As she approached even closer, she finally realized it was a small herd of wild ponies.

As she realized where the ponies were standing, Nina's heart lurched.

"My bike!" she cried, racing full tilt along the path, her footsteps like gunshots in the still island air.

The ponies backed away at her approach, nervously twitching their long, rough tails.

"Shoo! Shoo! Get away!" she told them firmly as she waved her arms.

Her bicycle, once a beautiful, shiny, metallic-green speedster, was now a trampled wreck. The sturdy little ponies were short but they weighed enough to do serious damage. As she inspected the much-abused bicycle, she also discovered they really *would* eat almost anything, as her heavy-duty tires had been nibbled to the point of uselessness.

"Oh no," she moaned, flopping to the sandy ground. Her

cottage was at least five miles away—a very long walk on a hot day.

She raised her head to discover that the ponies had formed a semicircle around her and were waiting as if to see what she was going to do. She had to laugh at their expectant faces.

"Thanks a lot, guys, you've really made my day," she told them, half-heartedly pitching a handful of sand at the cluster of muzzles.

One grizzled old fellow snorted loudly and tossed his pale mane as if telling her to pull herself up by her bootstraps and quit complaining.

"All right, I'm going," Nina replied, rising and dusting off the seat of her shorts.

The ponies moved back, stamping their feet and grunting, breath echoing in their lungs like a bellows. Greener grass beckoned and they began to disperse, prehensile lips and flat teeth ripping mightily at a new plot of drying marsh grass.

Nina plucked her twisted bike from the sand and stowed it behind a clump of bushes at the entrance to the trail. She would retrieve it later this evening in her car. She hoped it could be repaired. She glanced at the long stretch of highway curving off into the distance. If she ever made it home, that is.

She had walked only a few yards when a whizzing noise sounded behind her. A sudden gust of wind buffeted her as a biker, the same one who had passed her before, sped by.

Nina was thrown off balance by the passage and stumbled onto the sandy shoulder of the road. She cursed the biker soundly, her temper finally reaching the breaking point.

He must have heard her. To her dismay, he slowed and made a wide turn to come back to her.

Standing still, she dubiously watched his approach. She eyed the parking lot, about a half mile away, and wondered if anyone would hear if she screamed.

"I thought that was you." The biker stopped before Nina and stripped off his helmet. He was a her. And the her was Hazy.

Nina's mouth fell open in amazement and relief as she saw the familiar blond hair, now plastered to Hazy's skull with sweat, emerge from the hated black helmet. Nina's eyes took in the sweat-soaked, sleeveless T-shirt and the snug black Spandex shorts which hugged her lower body like a second skin. Surely this wasn't her temporary landlord. She seemed so young.

"What are you doing riding a bike?" she said, almost accusingly. "I thought boats were your favorite mode of transportation."

Hazy laughed and carefully hung the helmet on one handlebar by its chin strap. "Only at sea. On land I use whatever's handy." She added thoughtfully, "Although I guess I'll use whatever's handy at sea as well. I once floated on a barrel for four hours when my brother's science experiment failed."

Nina eyed her with doubt, afraid to ask about the experiment.

"The question that should be answered, I think, is why you are out walking in this heat." Hazy smiled as if she already knew the answer and Nina's anger began to rekindle.

"I don't see where that is any concern of yours, Ms. Duncan. I might be walking for exercise, you know." Her nose lifted just a smidgeon.

Hazy studied her coolly. "Hazy, I told you, or Hazel, if you feel a need to be formal. Well...if that be the case, I'll be off."

She placed one foot on a pedal and paused to study Nina again.

"Is your car nearby? I thought I saw it at the cottage when I left."

Nina was abruptly afraid Hazy would leave her here to make her own way home, but pride reared its head again. She always had a hard time asking for help.

"I was on a bike."

Hazy looked around. "Where is it then?"

"The ponies ate it."

Hazy became very still, as if her mind were turning over what Nina had told her.

"The ponies did what?"

74

Nina's face began to color as she realized how ridiculous she must sound. "The ponies ate my tires while I was on the nature trail."

Hazy began laughing then and Nina wasn't sure she was going to stop. She turned her back on Hazy and resumed walking along the road.

Finally the guffawing slowed and Hazy pulled up alongside Nina, balancing her weight easily on the well-maintained ten-speed. Stray chuckles still escaped every few seconds but she had herself under control.

"I'm glad some of us find it amusing," Nina told her in a frigid tone.

This almost set Hazy off again but she choked back the laughter and planted her feet on the ground so she could swipe at her weeping eyes.

"I've heard of a lot of strange happenings in my time, and the islands are full of strange happenings, but I'll admit this is a whole new one for me."

"Well, just zip on home and give the local newspaper a call," Nina snapped as she walked along, her stomping feet creating small dust clouds in the sand.

Hazy, rolling the bike slowly behind her, spoke softly. "I think it'd be best if we got you home first, don't you?"

"Do you have a car?" she asked, finally stopping to catch her breath. Walking along in the thick sand of the shoulder in this heat was making her heart rate increase.

"Yes, a Jeep. Why?"

Her eyes widened in exasperation. "Would you consider going to get the car and then coming back to pick me up?"

"Why? I've got the bike right here. Hop on."

Nina's dark eyes roamed the sleek, streamlined machine. "There's no room."

"Don't be silly," she replied. "You're a slip of a thing and will fit right nicely up here on the handlebars."

Nina looked at the place she indicated, a small scooped-out

area between the two handles, and shook her head. "Nope. Won't work. You won't be able to see."

"Of course I can see. I'll just look around you. It's not but a few miles, gull."

Nina stamped her foot. "I am not a girl. I'm just small because I'm Irish. Don't call me a girl!"

Hazy spread both hands in defense. "All right, all right, I'm sorry. Don't get your feathers riled."

Nina glared at her. Hazy finally closed her eyes and sighed. "Look here, there's no sense fighting about this thing. You need a ride and I am offering one. You'll just have to trust me to know what I can and cannot handle on my own bike."

Nina was tired and common sense told her what Hazy was saying was the truth. Nevertheless, her superior attitude annoyed Nina and her pride smarted at being forced to accept her largesse.

"Fine. If you think you can control it and not kill us both then I guess I'll just have to take your word for it."

"Right," Hazy agreed. Throwing one smooth leg over the crossbar, she dismounted, handed Nina the bike and roughly pulled the pack from Nina's shoulders.

"Ow, that hurts," Nina cried, jerking her arm from the last loop. "Can't you be a little more gentle?"

"Well, it's not easy when you have to deal with women-shaped cacti who specialize in spitting you with spines every time you come near."

Nina turned to face Hazy, her features drawn into a scowl. "I haven't done a single, solitary thing to you. You just stay in a bad mood all the time and expect everyone to accept it as a matter of course. I personally don't like being around bad-tempered people."

"Then stay away from them. Besides, you've been pretty disagreeable today yourself."

"I guess so! Here I am, minding my own business, taking a few photos and wham! A herd of stubby horses tramples and eats my bike, leaving me to walk in hundred degree heat. This is not something guaranteed to make you shout with joy."

At the mention of the ponies Hazy's lips began to quiver and laughter threatened.

"Don't you dare!" Nina cautioned her.

Hazy ducked behind the bike and began deftly tying the pack onto it with elastic cords stowed in a compartment above the chain. When she stood, she was no longer laughing but her blue eyes were wet and gleeful. She buckled the straps of her sweaty helmet around the pack, apologizing for not having a dry one for Nina to wear.

"All right then, up with you," she said as she took the handlebars from Nina's hands. "I'll hold it steady."

Awkwardly, Nina hoisted herself onto the handlebars and settled her bottom into the middle. She fit well.

Hazy, with an alarming wobble, mounted and began rolling the bike forward slowly. She raised up and pushed hard on the right pedal and they were off.

Nina had ridden roller coasters. Nina had ridden sleds. Nina had even been skiing. But nothing could have prepared her for the reckless speeds Hazy Duncan attained on the trip home.

The small fresh- and salt-water ponds on either side of the road passed by in a frightening blur as she held on for dear life with both hands clenched around the handlebars at her sides and her hiking boots tucked back and around the bottom frame. Her hair felt as though it were being ripped from the top of her head and her eyes dried out as quickly as her eyelids could moisten them.

Though frightened to her wits' end, Nina found the ride exhilarating, leaning with Hazy as they rounded curves and laughing out loud in spite of her terror.

Hazy didn't slow appreciably until they started across the causeway onto Chincoteague where traffic was heavier.

"Wasn't it fun?" Hazy asked against her ear. She was breathing heavily but Nina could sense she was smiling, though whether from sheer enjoyment of the ride or glee from scaring Nina half to death she couldn't tell.

"I do this for exercise two days a week; spend half the day racing about the big island. Supposed to be good for me," she panted as they rounded onto Church Street.

"Yeah," Nina replied when she could catch her breath. "If you survive it."

Hazy chuckled and Nina found herself smiling.

They were at Channel Haven. Hazy held the bike steady as Nina dismounted, her legs shaking.

"What will you do about your bike? Leave it for dessert?"

Nina was uselessly trying to straighten her windblown hair but the words caused her to turn and eye Hazy angrily.

"You're making fun of me, aren't you?" she challenged her. "I didn't ask for any of this to happen and I think you're pretty rude to make jokes about it."

A familiar scowl darkened Hazy's perspiring face as she loosened the pack and handed it to her. "I think I deserve a few laughs after rescuing you."

"Rescuing me! You half-killed me. I thought I was dead when I saw you come within an inch of that red car making a turn." She was still shaking with fear but it had changed to a trembling of indignation.

"Why, you scared little ninny! You act like I've been riding for only a few months. I've been riding since before you were born and haven't had a spill yet."

"It's only a matter of time. Sooner or later your luck has got to run out. And you are careless about other people, you almost ran me down earlier today as well, on the main road." She fixed her in an angry stare.

Hazy studied her, turned away. "Perhaps if I'd done so, I wouldn't have had to waste the time bringing you back here."

Hazy swung onto her bike and pedaled off, leaving Nina standing in the driveway, infuriated.

Chapter 15

When Nina went to the office to fetch her mail the next morning, she was pleasantly surprised to find an unfamiliar middle-aged woman sitting at the big metal desk.

The woman, who possessed long dark red hair and snapping blue eyes, was big in body and big in smile.

"Hello there," she greeted Nina as she rose to shake her hand, "and who might you be?"

"Nina Christie," Nina responded quickly. So this must be Hazy's partner. "And you must be..."

"Carrie Newcomb, but everybody just calls me Mama New and you're to be no exception, hear?" She touched one forefinger to her chin and rolled her eyes as if searching the ceiling. "Christie, Christie. Seems I 'member the name. Didna' I talk to you on the phone once, some time ago?"

"Yes, this past week," Nina supplied, feeling comforted by the woman's island dialect. "I asked to rent a cottage while I waited for my house to be finished. I inherited Tom Burley's old place over on the North Channel."

"Oh, ta, I remember now," Mama New said as she resumed her seat, all the while talking amiably. "Sorry I wasn't here to tend to you and you had to deal with the madam Hazel. Ignore her right enough and you'll be the better for it."

She took a deep breath and jumped in again. "I suppose it could drive a body mad sitting here day after day dealing with the tourists and the business. So anyways, off I goes to get a little rest and relaxation at my sister's house in Stafford and she stays here and minds the phone and the baby. So off she goes now for the day, just to get in a bit of fishing and I fill in for her. After all, it's the least we can do, you know? The hardest part," she lowered her voice and leaned forward conspiratorially, "is keepin' the housekeepin' staff in line. When they see she's gone for the day, they like to be slack-abouts and not get their work done. The idiots should know her temper by now and how she'll bellow when she comes in an' sees the work left undone."

Mama New took a deep breath but before she could start up again, Nina, totally bewildered by the whole monologue, spoke up.

"Has a courier come, Mama New?" she asked. "I'm expecting an important package."

"Oh sure, honey, Lyle came by just a while ago." Mama New moved over to the wooden boxes filling one wall. Nina smiled at the unaffected way she stopped and adjusted her long flowing dress over her ample hips before crossing the room.

"Let's see, number eight, wasn't it? Or number twelve? There's something there too today." She peered curiously into the wooden latticework of mailboxes.

"Number eight," Nina replied, trying not to laugh at the woman's endearing mannerisms.

"Well, here you go then; a small stack." She handed it over to Nina then moved closer to read the return addresses as Nina leafed through them.

"Anything interesting?" she asked, curiosity emanating from her.

Nina groaned inwardly. Her days of freedom were over. A large white overnight delivery mailer from Jennings-Ryder Books was included and she knew herself well enough to know she would not be able to lay the manuscript aside. She'd have to read at least the first chapter to get the flavor of the novel before doing anything else.

A waybill copy was attached to the package and Nina touched it where Hazy's large sweeping signature flashed across it.

Since Mama New was still watching, Nina pulled out the small box sent from her father and opened it.

"Oh, a book," said Mama New. "Isn't that sweet. From a boyfriend perhaps?"

"Oh no," Nina answered quickly, "just my father. He always sends me stuff. I'm an only child and my parents tend to spoil me."

The admission, though she tried to make it nonchalant, had always come out a bit defensively. What right had she to receive the sole attention of two parents when other children had to share love and attention?

"Now that's a nice thing," said Mama New as she moved back to sit behind the desk. She lifted a hand up to pat the auburn hair coiled at the nape of her neck.

"Is ta hard being an only child? We have four but they've all moved away now 'cept for the little one, Heather. She's only five and is a handful enough. I don't think I had as much trouble with the four all at once as I do with this wee one alone." She paused and eyed Nina with one eye closed. "Do you think Heather will do all right being by herself now? I often wonder it, I do."

"I think so," Nina replied, thinking, four children! No wonder Hazy had to work so hard, especially if she was helping put some through college. "I've been happy and have always considered myself lucky not having to share my parents."

Mama New nodded her agreement and sighed. "I suppose

you're right, one can't help worrying though."

The door opened then and Hazy walked in, a fierce frown marring her features.

"Where is Eduardo?" she demanded of Mama New. "I've got three boats he was supposed to clean this mornin' and they haven't been touched. And Manny's off today."

Mama New came around the desk to soothe her partner. "Now Hazy, honey, let's not have a blow. Eduardo's gone over to south end to see about getting more vacuum bags for the gals so they can finish up the cottages. He'll be back shortly and I'll ride him hard 'till the work's done."

"Ah, I didn't realize. I thought he was just layin' out again," Hazy remarked somewhat sheepishly. "Sorry to take it out on you, love." She swung one arm about Mama New's shoulders and pulled her close.

Her eyes finally caught Nina standing by the dock door, mail cradled to her chest.

"What have ye done to your hair?" she asked abruptly. "Have ye cut it?"

Nina reached up a hand to pull the bulk of her ponytail from behind her back. She felt like a naughty child.

"Well thank goodness for that," she said, "but it's much more becomin' when it's down and loose."

Mama New looked from Nina to Hazy in confusion.

Hurt and indignant, Nina mumbled an excuse and slammed out the door. She stomped around the deck and across the drive, seeking the safety of her cottage.

How dare she treat her that way and in front of her partner! How could such a sweet woman stand to live with such a harridan?

Sitting at her desk, forcibly dismissing Hazy and Mama New from her mind, Nina took out the new Jennings-Ryder manuscript and tried to concentrate on it.

Written by a woman named Kathryn Shaner, the book, titled *Fate in her Hands* was, according to the summary, about a young woman who held her large family together through terrible odds, including a disastrous fire, the death of a patriarch, a kidnapping and a sea voyage.

She was caught up in the story for a short time but her mind kept wandering to the real drama outside the novel.

Putting the book aside, she pulled out the enclosed letter from Martha. In the missive, Martha stated that she was looking forward to visiting Nina's new home and seeing the ocean during her favorite ocean watching time, a heavy storm.

Nina dropped the letter and walked over to the far window to watch the dancing channel water.

Only to espy the woman who kept her emotions so stormy of late. She was cleaning her boats. Obviously, Eduardo had not yet returned, even though it was almost noon.

Nina watched the play of muscles under the skin of Hazy's thinly clad back as she stretched out an arm trying to scrub a faraway point on the stern of the little craft. Her hands were dripping and soapy and an unexpected thrill went through Nina as soapsuds ran down her arm and trickled along to dampen the shirt above her well-defined ribs.

Enough!

Nina couldn't believe she was lusting so after someone—a married someone at that. And someone almost twice her age. It was totally unlike her and she had to put a stop to it.

Donning a light shirt over her T-shirt and shorts, Nina left the cottage and got into her car. Maybe spending some money would make her feel better.

Chapter 16

Hazy straightened from the crouched position she had assumed next to the rental boat she was cleaning and surreptitiously watched Nina leave the cottage. Nina didn't even glance her way as she got into and drove off in her little bubble car.

She wanted to go after her, to soothe the anger and hurt somehow. She was afraid though, afraid she would be unable to choose the right words.

No, actually she was afraid of what might spew uncontrolled from her damning mouth.

She smiled ruefully at the smooth, white side of the small two-seater and ran her hand slowly across its broad, wet sleekness, imagining it as Nina's skin.

She might accidentally tell Nina she wanted her. Maybe even that she might fall in love with her if she spent too much time alone with her. And that would be almost worse than dying because then she'd have to deal with her feelings...and Nina's feelings.

Her gaze traveled along the road in the direction Nina had gone.

She was too fetching a woman. Dressed in shorts she showed a little more leg and appeared more grown up. Dressed in her usual denims and T-shirts, her tiny size made her look like a prepubescent teen and Hazy felt every year of their age difference when next to her. It was hard enough taking her eyes off Nina when she was wearing jeans. Dressed as she was now, well...Her mind drifted to the overwhelming attraction she had felt for her a few nights before.

There must have been some erotic quality in the fact that she had just come from the bath. Or perhaps it came from being in the close confines of that tiny room together...her lemony soap smell...just the two of them amid the silence of the night.

She slapped the side of the boat then turned and pressed the hot skin of her cotton-clad back against its wet coolness. Leaning her head back, she shut her eyes tight, enjoying the heat of the sun on her skin. She was acting like a mesmerized schoolgirl, filled with the ache of longing.

For many years now, she had avoided true intimacy. But avoiding closeness with Nina was taking every ounce of prickly fortitude she had in her. She still wasn't sure what specifically had prevented her from going to Nina and laying lips against the gentle pulse that moved under the curve of her neck.

When Nina had come looking for help, Hazy had just finished dinner with Heather and had tucked her in. During dinner, she'd had a couple glasses of the fine German wine brought to her long ago by her friend, Seth. This had prompted maudlin thoughts about Seth's death.

Then Nina had arrived with her talk of books and authors. Hazy had dreamed for a very short while that Nina could fill that lonely gap that devoured her from the inside out. She had begun to see her as a comrade and that was very dangerous indeed.

She actually enjoyed being with Nina and this was something she could say about few women she'd met in her life.

It had embarrassed her this morning when she'd been so mean to her in front of Mama New. The hardest part had been trying to explain it to Carrie without letting her know she'd been smitten by Nina. How could she tell her that being mean to Nina was her only defense? How could she explain that if she was the least bit nice, too much emotion would come out, deflating her like a rubber balloon? Carrie would think her crazy. She already did, it seemed like.

She sighed wearily. All she could do now was stay as far as possible from Miss Nina Christie and hope desperately that her house would be finished sooner rather than later.

She turned back to the boat and, using pent-up emotion and confusion as a spur, began furiously scrubbing it to pristine whiteness.

Chapter 17

The day had grown hot while she'd been cooped up inside her cottage. Beach Road had a good layer of heat vapor rising from it. The ocean breezes didn't reach this far inland and the middle of the island simmered in the August sunlight.

Nina parked her Volkswagen before a small independent grocery and, stripping off her light overshirt, stepped into the brutal sunlight. Across the street a small fair had been set up in a wooded grove but few people were out braving the heat.

Trying to keep her mind occupied, she went into the store and bought a few nonperishable provisions. The high point of the excursion was discovering the grocery stocked her favorite brand of shampoo.

Gasping as she stepped back into the late summer heat from the coolness of the grocery store, Nina stowed the items in the back of her car and strolled over to the fair.

Tables had been set up on a lawn that was remarkably green

for August and about a dozen local crafters were displaying their handiwork. Many artisans actually were practicing their craft, working so a mere fair would waste no time. An elderly gentleman who was carving ducks and other waterbirds from blocks of pale wood piqued her interest. Several of the birds, painted in muted, natural colors rested on a nearby table.

Intrigued, Nina lifted one and was amazed by its realistic appearance.

"Looks fair ready to take to the water, doesn't it, miss?" The man paused in his carving and watched her with avid curiosity. "These were used as decoys back when hunting meant dinner on the table. Ducks are stupid but sly. How real your bird looked decided whether you ate that night," he told her cheerfully.

Nina smiled, enchanted by the gentleman. "Well, you've done a fine job. I bet you've never gone hungry."

He laughed and slapped a hand on his thigh. "Thank you, miss, but that's not the case. I was lazy as a boy and when I didn't fetch the birds fast enough for my da, I went hungry no matter how many ducks he brought home for the pot."

Nina looked at him in surprise. "That's not very nice."

He shrugged and bent back to his carving. "I learned not to be lazy."

He peered up at her. "Where are you from? You look like someone I know."

"I'm from Alexandria actually, but my Grandpapa Tom lived here and I used to visit him from time to time."

"Tom, Tom who?" he asked, squinting one eye to peer up at her.

"Tom Burley, over on the channel," she replied.

"Sure, I know who you're talkin' about. I served as mate under Captain Tom on the *Lady Say*. I seen your likeness on the mantel board at the big house one day. That's why I thought you looked familiar. You look a little like your mother, too. I knew Miss Emily, you know, and her passing was a harsh blow to us all. I thank ye that Tom had the gull Freda to look after."

Nina was delighted to find someone new who worked with her grandfather. The man, who she soon discovered was named Cyrus Leppard, entertained her with tales of the sea and of her grandfather when he was a young man.

As the sun's rays lengthened along the grass of the park, Cyrus brought Nina over to a group of retired locals gathered there at the fair, all of whom had been peers of her grandfather and who further entertained her with her grandfather's exploits.

One story, obviously a favorite, concerned the storm of 1944 when Tom had been a young hand on another's fishing boat.

"I remember it like yesterday," Cyrus began. "We'd gone out for a load of bluegill for Handy Thomas…"

"You all remember Handy's restaurant, there on Pikes Street?" Sheltie Pierce asked, removing his cigarette from his mouth and gesturing east with it.

A communal nod and murmur sounded and Nina smiled. The restaurant was way before her time but she remembered Sheltie. Her grandfather had taken her with him often to Sheltie's small camper on Little Oyster to pick up fresh shrimp or a late summer alewife for dinner.

"Wadn't he wiped out by Connie in fifty-five?" a grizzled man asked. He had a neck that resembled folded leather.

"Yep, ta one. So even though it was nigh on to fall, Handy had a hankerin' to run a special on bluegill. So out we goes, a five-man crew…"

"Three sheets to the wind, as was the way," offered another old salt as he removed his cap and scratched his balding head.

The others laughed as Nina tried to place the phrase. One sailor noted her confusion and mimed drinking from a bottle. Nina blushed and chuckled.

"Well, it had turned a might chill," Cyrus muttered in the crew's defense before continuing. "Back then, they never said naught about the blows coming up the seaboard, so we goes out all happy on Jackson Reed's fishing scow and some was playing gin in the hold, never noting the storm skies at all. Then lookout calls and we rush up and ta squall's on us…"

"Thirty-foot swells reach up before we knowed," commented Sheltie, "and we all falls back and are swimmin' aboard…"

"That we were," agreed Cyrus with an expansive nod. "So young Tom's hanging on to the mains'l, feet to the wind and up comes the man boat, damn near slams him, and who's hidin' under it but Charlie Gaynes and his gullfriend, Tabitha."

The men laughed as one as Cyrus continued. "So Tabby grabs onto Tom's legs and she's crawlin' up him as Charlie hangs on to the boat for all he's worth."

"So we got Tom and Tabby on the mains'l, Charlie on the rowboat holdin' by one line. We got Cy and Jimmy over there port and starboard, and me and Jackson aft, all hangin' on for dear life," added Sheltie.

"And the wind, she blowed," continued Cyrus. "When she died a bit, we took stock and Tom, ever ta gennelman, set Tabby down easy and helped Charlie secure the second line on the man boat. Just as they finished, here she comes again, right over the deck. So's we all grab aholt again and the boat, she be spinnin' around. I look over and Tabby's got the mains'l now with Tom and Charlie a hangin' offa her."

"And next we know, off comes ta gull's skirt, bloomers and all. Tom flies with 'em but nabs the riggin' and Charlie fetches up against ta rail, ta gull's bloomers in his hand," Sheltie slapped his thigh and led the appreciative laughter.

Gasping with merriment, Cyrus continued, "There she is, flyin' from the mains'l like a pirate's pennant, white nether cheeks shining through the dark." He snorted with laughter, waving his hands as if drawing the image. "Tom sees what's happened and he's fightin' the wind to get to Tabby but it's hard goin.' He hand-over-hands the riggin,' makin' his way to the mains'l. He somehow pulls her down and they crawl on they's bellies to the hold and spill over in with the waterfall."

"An' we never let him forget the day," added Sheltie. "We rode out the storm, all lookin' like drowned rats when ta's over.

Took us a week to bail out the hold but ever' time we worked it we had to laugh at Tom and that pretty white bottom spillin' over in."

"Poor Tabby," Cyrus said, chuckling. "She was never able ta look straight on at any of us after that."

Laughing, Sheltie, motioned with one hand. "The boat, tell 'bout ta boat."

Cyrus laughed and mopped at his eyes with both gnarled hands. "Jackson christen'd the boat again after ta re-work. Made Tom do it with a bottle of elderberry wine. He called it...called it...the *Broken Moon*."

Nina laughed along with the rest of them even as another tale was begun. By late afternoon, when she helped Cyrus load his truck for home and waved a farewell, Nina felt as though she knew her grandfather as she never had before.

After popping back into the store to purchase bottled iced tea, Nina drove toward Channel Haven, her mind relaxed and filled with fondness, lingering on her grandfather's life.

Chapter 18

The familiar blue truck parked in front of her cottage door wiped away the mists of the past. As she parked her car next to it, she was able to see the driver. Mander.

Groaning inwardly, she looped her plastic grocery bags over her arm and rose clumsily from the car.

Mander shouted a cheery hello from the open truck window. "I thought you might like a little company tonight," she called. "See? I brought wine." She held up a dark green bottle and wagged it back and forth.

Nina was disarmed by her enthusiasm and smiled.

Taking this as encouragement, Mander leapt from the vehicle and waited with an anxious air in front of the cottage door. She appeared to be fresh from the shower, her hair still damp, and she wore a Hawaiian-styled shirt and denim shorts.

Nina sighed with something akin to vexation but nevertheless moved to the door and ushered her in.

As Nina put away her purchases, Mander roamed the small cottage, criticizing the poor construction points which had totally escaped Nina's notice. She had thought the small house charming and so her reply was caustic.

"I suppose you'll just have to offer your services to Ms. Duncan so some measure of perfection can be obtained."

Mander's puzzled frown quickly faded and she answered, "You're right, I should. Old man Leppard and his cronies had a part in building this place and none of them have a reputation for framing a house plumb."

Nina busied herself folding the cumbersome grocery bags so the other woman couldn't see her annoyance. Was she talking about the kind woodcarver she'd met earlier that day? She hoped not, for she had no wish to argue that point with Mander. In fact, she was beginning to heartily wish she'd just go home and leave her to the peace of the ocean.

The ocean. Perhaps she could divert Mander as well as herself.

"Mander," she said, turning from the cabinets. "Why don't you and I go and sit on the dock. We could relax and talk out there."

Mander was opening the wine. Fetching two glasses from the cupboard, she replied, "Oh no, let's stay inside. The wind is up and I'd much rather be cozy in here with you." She moved close and handed her a full glass of rose-colored wine. "Let's sit here on the sofa and talk a little."

Mander proceeded to take a seat in the center of the sofa and took a long swallow of the wine.

Nina could not tolerate sitting so close. Stalling, she tasted the wine, then crossed to the door and looked out across the channel. The lighthouse had just come to life and was winking cheerily at her from the other island.

It made her feel unaccountably sad, a deep sense of loneliness washing over her. She sighed. Maybe she was simply feeling sorry for herself because of Rhonda's poor treatment of her.

With a start, she realized Mander had been talking for some time.

"...and I really would like to see us develop a close relationship. I'm sure it would be satisfying to both of us."

"Who?" interjected Nina with some alarm.

"Why us, you and me," Mander answered, looking at her in momentary confusion. "Look." She raised her hands, palms toward Nina, the glass of wine held precariously between thumb and forefinger of her right hand. "I know what you said the other day, about not wanting this, but once you get used to me and to living here on the island, you'll be fine. Why don't you let me help you get over Tom's death and this bad relationship you've had? I can make you happy, you know I can."

Nina was touched as well as bothered by her speech and still couldn't bring herself to sit next to her.

She turned her attention back to the light and spoke slowly, thoughtfully.

"It's not a matter of making me happy, Mander. I am happy, basically. I do hope to settle down someday but right now I'm being cautious. I've been hurt..."

"Well, so have I," Mander interrupted quickly. "Most people have. You've just got to get over it and go on with your life. Being alone is not the answer."

"That's not always so," Nina protested hotly, "sometimes being alone can be a much-needed time of healing. And that healing is what I feel I need right now."

Mander said, "I really feel you need someone you can be with to help you over the bad times. I've given this a lot of thought and I'm sure I'm right."

Nina was angered and her voice was clenched as she answered. "Who are you to know what I want, Amanda Sheridan? I am Nina, not Mander, and I feel what Nina feels, not what Mander feels. Surely you have enough intelligence to realize that?"

If Mander was taken aback by her tone it was not for long. She crossed the room to her. "Come on, Nina, just give it a try.

You'll see I'm right." She wrapped an arm about her shoulders.

Nina immediately moved away. "Just stay away from me, Mander. I've asked you nicely not to push me. I need time. Any hope of our having some type of friendly relationship depends on you respecting my wishes."

"But Nina," she pleaded, moving slowly toward her. "Let's just hang out together, get closer, give it a try."

"Mander." Nina's voice was cool steel and had a deadly ring. "If you come any closer, you'll get this glass of wine full in the face. I am not kidding."

Mander paused and eyed the upraised glass uncertainly.

A firm knock at the screen door broke the tension. Nina moved to the door.

Hazy stood just outside, hands in the pockets of her denim shorts and her head and neck tucked down into her open collar like an apologetic child.

"Hello Hazy," Nina said gratefully. "What can I do for you?"

"Need to check that stem so I can order the right knob from the mainland is all," she told her, squinting up from her position at the bottom of the steps.

Nina, silent a moment, suddenly realized the woman was aware of the problem she was having with Mander.

Hazy smiled as if she sensed Nina's realization and Nina returned the smile with unusual warmth.

"Come on in," she invited, standing aside.

Hazy's presence filled the small room then and she nodded politely to Mander.

She moved on to the bathroom and Mander, visibly miffed by the entire turn of events, slammed her wineglass onto the table, muttered a farewell and stomped off.

Nina collapsed onto the sofa with a deep sigh.

Hazy found her there a few moments later.

"Comfortable, are you?" she asked, a grin highlighting her features.

Nina smiled warily, wondering what sarcasm was coming

next. "Yes, glad to relax. It's been quite a day."

"Umm hmm," she agreed. "Well, I'll be off now." She moved across the room and opened the screen door.

"Hazy." Nina said the name softly. "Thank you very much."

Hazy turned and gave Nina one of her rare warm smiles as she left.

Chapter 19

Much later that evening, as stars and wispy clouds decorated the night sky, a restless Nina wandered out to the boat rental docks.

The tide was high and little sea creatures of all types were skittering over the lower dock which was already covered by shallow water.

Aimlessly, Nina strolled along the waterfront toward the office and its attached dock. She passed one young couple who greeted her, but otherwise had the night all to herself.

Walking toward the office, Nina entertained thoughts of Hazy. She half wanted Hazy to join her here on the dock, to have her standing there with her listening to the slap and whisper of the waves caressing the wooden planks.

But how could she want this—the woman was a complete bitch, a woman who absolutely hated the rest of humanity. And she belonged to someone else. There was Mama New and the children they had. The children they were raising together.

She leaned her forearms on the railing and let the heated ocean breeze waft through her hair and T-shirt. Why did she feel drawn to Hazy in such a way? Never had she felt such a deep and inexplicable attraction. It seemed as if it were manifesting on some primal level, one that had never before surfaced. Rhonda, over a period of years, had certainly never touched a level that Hazy had, and during just the past few days.

Subtle sounds behind her made her aware that Hazy had come onto the dock. Nina closed her eyes and held her breath. She really didn't need to see her right now when she was feeling so vulnerable. She stiffened her resolve. She'd just have to remain uninvolved and ignore that part of herself that yearned for Hazy.

"Care for an ale?" Hazy asked, joining her at the railing and offering a dark bottle of beer.

Nina accepted it with a mere nod and they watched the night ocean together in silence.

After both bottles were almost empty, Hazy stretched her arms high over her head.

"How about a swim while the water's warm?" she suggested, inclining her head toward the water.

Nina smiled and nodded. "I'll run and get into my suit."

"Ah no," Hazy said, her tone arresting Nina as she moved toward her cottage. "That's not the way you enjoy the ocean."

Nina searched for merriment and found it dancing in Hazy's blue eyes.

"You mean…"

"Aye, gotta go buck naked to get the full benefit."

"Ha," Nina barked, "you've lost your mind."

Hazy stood back, arms crossed across her chest, and studied the younger woman. "So, what are you hidin', little miss?"

"Why, nothing," Nina protested. "I'm just not going to take my clothes off in front of a stranger."

"I'm not that strange," Hazy replied. She was in a teasing mood and Nina found it disturbing—in a good way. Hazy reached out and gently tugged at her shirt.

"You know, even if you swim in your undies, you'll probably be better covered than most of the ladies paradin' around Assateague Beach."

Nina was weakening under this new charming Hazy. Besides, what she said was true, her undershirt and panties certainly covered more skin than most bathing suits. Her long undershirt would cover more than her modest one-piece suit.

"All right, you're on," she said, grinning and unbuttoning her shorts.

Hazy answered with a grin of her own and peeled her T-shirt over her head, revealing a ribbed muscle shirt.

Nina, after dropping her shorts and taking off her own outer shirt, eyed her curiously. "Well, aren't you going to take off your shorts?" she asked finally.

Hazy's eyes twinkled merrily in the twilight as if she were thoroughly relishing her next statement.

"That's as far as I can go, ducks, unless you give me the okay. No panties."

She slowly reached for the waistband of her shorts but Nina stopped her.

"Oh no, that's fine, as long as you get the 'benefit' of the water," she replied with pointed sarcasm.

They raced for the edge of the dock but Hazy was first to dive into the warm channel water. Nina followed, diving cleanly into the churning waves.

Hazy surfaced next to her, hair made sleek and darker by the water. Her white teeth gleamed in the beam from the lighthouse. Nina swiped at her face and grinned as she treaded water. "God, this feels good."

"See yonder buoy?" Hazy said pointing. "I'll meet you there."

Nina peered into the dimness. The buoy looked tiny in the distance. She wasn't sure she could make it. She glanced back at Hazy and saw the challenge in her gaze.

"All right, then," she said, accepting the dare. "You're on."

Nina enjoyed the sleek caress of the waves as her arms speared through the water. And though she sped through as fast as she was able, Hazy waited for her, one arm strung nonchalantly through the buoy struts.

Panting, Nina tried to grasp the buoy but her hands slipped off and she went under. Hazy grabbed her around the waist and hoisted her higher so she could reach the metal supports. She brushed the hair from Nina's face.

"You okay, ducks?"

Nina saw the concern in Hazy's eyes and something in her melted. Unable to speak, she only nodded.

They hung there many minutes in silence, the ocean rocking them as gently as any mother. When the buoy had sounded a dozen times, Hazy sighed. "I guess we'd better get back."

The return swim to Channel Haven was leisurely, part of it spent floating on their backs. Hazy never left her side.

Gaining the dock, Nina swung herself onto the lowest step and, cradling her knees to her chest, wrapped her arms around them.

Air hot but half an hour ago was now cool on her sea-dampened skin and she shivered.

Hazy, who had followed Nina in, climbed past her and onto the landing. She returned moments later and wrapped a large, thick towel around Nina's shoulders.

Smiling her gratitude, Nina cuddled into the towel and stared at the lighthouse which every moment or so bathed her in a blushing, yellow glow.

They sat in companionable silence for a long while but soon the memory of sleek, strong thighs glimpsed in passing began to impact Nina. Restlessly she shifted position, trying to jog her mind back to the beauty of the scene before her.

"Are you cold?" Hazy asked. "Need a second towel?"

Why did she have to be so blasted solicitous all of a sudden? This was infinitely worse than dealing with her as an ogre. Nina didn't know how to react.

"No, I'm fine, thanks," she choked out between teeth

chattering from frustration as much as from the chill.

"Here." Hazy moved close behind her and using her own towel, began to gently dry Nina's hair by caressing it with the soft cloth.

Nina, blanking out everything, leaned back between the outspread knees and allowed the pleasurable sensation to wash over her. The small voice of reason hit her and her eyes snapped open. Mama New or anyone else could be watching them from any window.

She pulled away and whirled to face Hazy. "Please, what are you doing?"

Hazy watched Nina, her expression gentle and soft. "What is it?"

Nina was at a loss. There was a war raging within, between sensation and common sense. She was sincerely beginning to doubt her sanity. How could she let herself be so easily swept away by this manic woman?

Then Hazy leaned forward and pressed a soft kiss to Nina's trembling lips.

Nina pulled back, escaping Hazy for a moment, but Hazy stayed close, so close their breath mingled then captured her lips again. The kiss was gentle but possessive and the combination of Hazy's tongue and firm mouth ignited a slumbering giant within Nina.

Nina could only respond. She felt drugged by Hazy's nearness, her head swimming from a sudden onslaught of pounding blood in her veins. Crisp, startling fear was engulfing her as well; the fear of losing control and the resultant havoc this could bring to her calm, healing life.

Hazy pulled back and studied the face so close to her own. Her gentle expression changed, became hooded.

"Oh, hey, I'm sorry, Nina. I lost control. Too much ale, too much...I da know."

Nina could not reply but after a brief time was able to rise on wobbly legs. She pushed past Hazy, grabbed her clothing and raced to her cottage, the towel floating to the dock behind her.

Chapter 20

Although Nina tried very hard to read and critique the Shaner novel the next morning, her head just wasn't into it.

Erotic images of Hazy Duncan's face just an inch from her own, of those strong, tanned thighs pressing close to Nina's shoulder as Hazy moved the towel across her hair, the hot beer-scented breath across and in her mouth—these sensual images kept her distracted from the task before her.

She was bewildered by her reactions to this enigmatic woman. Nina seemed to have no control when she was near, no sense of propriety, and this shocked her. What had happened to the self-contained, controlled person she always believed she was?

Hazy Duncan. It was her fault.

Nina strode to the screen door and watched as her tormenter carefully applied a coat of blue paint to the equipment shed across and to her left.

The rogue was probably toying with her deliberately as she'd heard many married women on the prowl were wont to do. It was classic stereotyping, like a dime-store novel, and Nina felt soiled for having been a part of it.

She watched Hazy's every move as she applied the paint in a slow, orderly fashion. She seemed thoughtful, emanating a calm, peaceful manner and Nina suddenly found it hard to color her as blackly as she deserved.

Or did she act the part well? An outside observer might think she wasn't even attached to Mama New. Nina knew better though; she'd witnessed the closeness of their bond and the way Hazy acted with her partner and with Heather. This seemed to be a lovely relationship and being with Heather certainly brought out Hazy's beautiful mothering side.

A new idea interjected itself. Why had Hazy let her see their closeness? A sudden scowl twisted her features. Why had she been so mean to Nina about her hair? The answer was now obvious.

It was a ploy to keep her partner in the dark about her infidelities and clearly she wanted Nina to accept this marriage and still dally with her on the side.

Because of Rhonda, Nina was vulnerable right now. That's how Hazy had managed to squirm her way into her sensibilities. Rhonda had done much more than just leave her at the altar, she had left her with a vulnerability that vultures like Hazy Duncan could feast upon.

Moving back again to the kitchen table, she idly fingered the manuscript as her mind again relived the delicious events of the previous evening.

Sighing in frustration, she left the work and changed into her swimsuit. Maybe some sun and sea would cleanse her mind.

Hazy heard Nina leave the cottage via slamming the door and her heart dropped low in her chest. She was still angry, no doubt about that now.

Hazy had debated going to her and apologizing, wanting to

somehow bring Nina's dimpled smile back. Embarrassment kept her away, also procrastination over doing something so awkward. Now it was too late.

Her chin fell and she let out a breath slowly. She never should have lost control that way. But there seemed to be no help for it.

Actually she had wanted to do much more and had to forcibly hold herself in check. What was it about Nina that drew her mind and her body so strongly?

She idly rolled the paint roller back and forth in the pan of paint as she reflected. Perhaps it was because she finally found a woman she had no desire to dissect. She really enjoyed Nina the way she was. Her mind was agile, giving back as good as she got, her emotions were volatile and would certainly never bore Hazy, and her body was as close to perfection as anyone could want.

Most importantly, they seemed to share many of the same interests and had this strong but mysterious chemistry between them. She'd never felt its like before and the novelty excited and puzzled her. It had created in her a deep desire to see where the chemistry would lead.

She carefully spread paint along the weathered boards of the equipment shed, her hands tremulous from the power of her thoughts.

Maybe she should simply indulge this desire. She was long overdue a chance at true love and passion.

A shout from the channel drew her attention and her heart leapt to her throat and fear made sudden sweat dapple her brow as she thought for a moment it was her friend Seth calling to her from the grave—a grave in the guise of a small silver motorboat.

The hailer shouted again and Hazy realized it was only Kerry Clark, younger son of one of the local families. Waving, Hazy walked to the edge of the boat dock and beckoned Kerry to come ashore.

Kerry shook his white-blond head and his large teeth flashed in a smile as he beckoned Hazy to come to him.

Hazy started to walk away and playfully ignore the boy but

instead threw caution to the winds. Stripping off her shoes she took a running leap and cannonballed into the lapping waves. Long strokes of her powerful arms soon had her next to the small craft and she greeted Kerry as she swiped water from her face.

"I didn't think you'd do it, ye damn fool," Kerry said, shaking his head in amazement. "You're still as crazy as you ever were."

He sobered as he studied the older woman's face. "It's good to see you, Hazy. And good to see you finally got a bit of the life back in you."

Hazy grabbed hold of the side of the small boat with both hands and began rocking it sharply back and forth trying to unseat the youth. "I'll show you life," she cried, laughing.

"Hey!" Kerry laughed, trying to hold onto fishing gear, beer cooler and boat all at the same time. "What'd I say, sheesh!"

"Is that life enough for you?" asked Hazy as she finally let the boat settle.

"You better leave me alone or I won't tell you about the shark Billy killed over in Tom's Cove," Kerry warned.

"A shark in the cove. No lie?" Hazy's interest was piqued.

She heaved herself into the boat and the two shared shark stories for some time, allowing Hazy a momentary distraction from soft brown hair and lively coffee-colored eyes.

When Hazy finally eased herself back over the side to return to Channel Haven, Kerry reminded her cheerfully. "See you at Dad's party tonight."

Hazy had promised to go to the function several weeks ago yet had forgotten about it until this moment. She groaned inwardly. She was in no mood for partying, but politeness demanded she attend. "See you at eight sharp," she told Kerry and made toward shore.

As her arms knifed the water and propelled her home, Hazy reconsidered her attitude toward the party. Maybe going out for an evening—something she hadn't done in a while—would be good for her. Seeing old friends she had been avoiding might be fun, and she could catch up on news from the local grapevine.

She'd arrange for a sitter for Heather and take Mama New. She'd really enjoy it.

She smiled and tucked her face into the soft, foamy water. If she kept on like this, she'd ruin her reputation as a crotchety, old recluse.

Chapter 21

Assateague Island beach was surprisingly crowded but Nina soon found her own special niche and settled in to enjoy the sun.

For some time she lost herself in the book her father had sent, an anthology of the past year's best science fiction stories. But several stories in a row bored her, being rehashes of old ideas and she soon let the book drop to the sand.

Restless, she sought the water and fought the powerful ocean waves until she was bone weary. Then she lazily scouted for shells, scarce this late in the day. The sun beating on her shoulders warmed her completely and the exertion eased a mind that had been sorely troubled of late. Toward sunset, she left the beach humming a happy tune.

As she reached the top of the wooden steps leading to the parking area, she came face to face with Mander.

"Well, hello," Mander said, "I hoped I might find you here when I didn't see your car at Channel Haven."

"Well, hello yourself," Nina replied teasingly. She was in such a relaxed mood she was able to forgive and forget their argument of the night before. "How long have you been looking for me?"

"This is the third rise I've climbed. I was about ready to give up and go without you."

"Go? Go where?"

"To a party on a friend's houseboat. Are you up for it?" She watched Nina expectantly.

In good spirits, Nina decided to agree. "Sure, it sounds like fun. One thing though, you have to keep your hands to yourself. We'll go as friends only, all right?"

Mander frowned at her bluntness. "Okay, whatever you say," she agreed with a dramatic sigh.

"Do I have time to go back to the cottage and change first?" Nina asked looking down at her wet, sand-spattered suit.

"Oh yeah, I told you we're not time-conscious on the island," she replied with a grin.

"You say this friend lives in a houseboat?" Nina asked as they meandered slowly through the parking lot toward her car. "I've never been on a houseboat before."

"A lot of people live in houseboats here. Rental and home prices are steep on Chincoteague—there's only so much land on an island. With houseboats, people can just pay rent on a shoreline or dock and tie up. I thought about doing it myself. As soon as my lease is up, I might."

She grimaced at Nina. "I rent an attic apartment from my parents and you can imagine how hard that is for a young out and about lesbo such as myself."

Nina laughed aloud. "Yes, I can see how that would be a problem. I can sympathize too, I've lived near my parents since I've been out of school. They don't bother me too much though, we're very close. They accept my lifestyle completely. Finally."

They paused next to Nina's Volkswagen and Mander opened the door for her.

"Listen, since your car is here, I'll stop for some food to take and meet you back at your cottage, okay?"

They shared a smile of truce. Nina knew there was the chance of peace between them at last and that felt good.

Chapter 22

Even though Nina was dressed simply in a soft summer dress of pale blue, the blessing of the sun had done its magic. She knew she looked particularly good that evening. Mander seemed impressed by the transformation and puffed up a bit as they paraded in front of her friends.

Aaron Clark, owner of the houseboat and their host for the evening, was an eccentric but lovable painter well into his sixtieth year, Mander had informed her. He was a large, graying man, roughened by the sea. Nina could tell he was from one of the original island families just by his appearance and mannerisms. He certainly didn't fit her impression of the successful highbrow artist. Clark reminded her more of the stereotypical grizzled sea captain. Much like her Grandpapa Tom.

Lamed by a leg injury, he held a type of court as he limped through the boat. The houseboat was large and already packed with a mass of noisily conversing people. They appeared to be tourists and locals alike.

Obviously, Aaron Clark, as an artist, was much in demand. His many paintings, scattered about the houseboat walls and stacked atop one another at the foot of each wall, were mostly landscapes and seascapes, but a few of his abstract pieces featuring the local marshes intrigued Nina.

The view from the spacious houseboat pleased her as well. Docked at The Burne Marina, the vessel faced a wide expanse of Chincoteague Bay with its darker waters and unadulterated, lighter breezes.

When Nina and Mander had entered the houseboat, Clark had taken her hand in both his knobby, arthritic hands, which still bore traces of hard-to-remove paint, and turned her slowly side to side so he could examine her.

"Well now, aren't you a lovely thing? What on earth are you doing with Miss Mander here? I can fix you up with ten men better an escort than her without even trying."

Mander smiled at the old man with good humor as she straightened the waistband of her walking shorts. "Topping the list would be your oldest boy, I'm sure. Face it, Aaron, Harry just doesn't want to get married."

Clark grinned like a small boy. "Can't fault an old coot for trying, now can you? I sure would like to see a grandchild before I pass on." He turned to Nina. "How do you feel about pale blondes, my dear?"

Nina's thoughts flew to Hazy and it took several awkward seconds before she realized he meant his son. "Oh, I..." she stammered mindlessly.

"That's quite all right, my dear," he said, seeing her bewilderment. "I forget you're not from these parts. You two go on and enjoy yourselves. There's plenty of food and drink." His voice trailed off and he had moved away from them into the crowd.

"So, want to lay bets on how stupid he thinks I am?" Nina whispered to Mander with a sigh.

Mander laughed and took Nina's hand, pulling her into the crowd. "I wouldn't worry about Aaron, Nina. The only thing he notices on a long-term basis is his painting. That's why he's been so successful, even in places like New York. If ever a man was obsessed with his work, that's Aaron."

Nina and Mander were soon separated when Aaron returned and whisked Nina off for introductions and Nina felt silly for worrying.

Nina was pleasantly surprised to see many of the older men she had chatted with at the crafter's fair, including Cyrus Leppard. He raised a toast to her in greeting as Aaron introduced the group. Mama New was there as well, dressed in a lovely teal pantsuit. She was ensconced amid the sailors, conversing brightly and Nina thought her a rose among thorns.

After much small talk in which she found herself telling her life story over and over again to each new acquaintance, Nina was finally allowed a respite and wandered aimlessly, admiring Aaron's works that peppered the houseboat.

Something nagged at her as she studied one of the more abstract of the pieces, but she felt at a loss to pinpoint the vision. The picture was in deep shades of red and purple with a center semicircle of pale flesh color.

"Do you like that one?" Aaron said as he came up behind her, his cane brushing gently against the worn floorboards.

"I like it very much," admitted Nina, "but there's something about it. What am I missing?"

Aaron laughed with keen amusement and laid one long-fingered hand on her forearm. "How perceptive you are, little Nina—little Grace. Did you know your name is Russian?"

"No, I didn't," she admitted with a shy grin. "My Irish father will love that when I tell him."

"Yes." The old man nodded knowingly. "Nina is Russian for Anne and Anne means 'little Grace.' Now there's a bit of trivia for you to file away."

He turned back to the artwork. "About the painting, there *is*

112

something there that is hard to grasp. May I?"

He pulled gently on her right hand, moving it toward the painting. At Nina's bemused nod, he traced the tips of her fingers gently over the canvas, beginning with the flesh-colored arc. As Nina watched, their hands outlined a lovely dark-haired, tawny-skinned woman lying in the shadows of the deep purples and reds. The flesh-colored area was her bare hip and flank caught in a spot of very bright, localized light.

"Do you see her? My wife?" he asked softly.

"Yes, yes, I do," Nina whispered. "She's lovely."

He released her hand. "Dead these many years but she was quite a woman. Full of mystery, like this painting."

Nina's hand reached again to explore the mystery as Clark wandered away.

"It took me many hours to figure it out," said a soft voice behind her.

The voice sent a small shiver along her spine, a shiver that reached up and tightened the muscles of her face. She didn't even bother to turn. "Hello, Hazy. How are you?"

"Not bad for a woman getting older every day. And you?"

Nina smiled at the painting. "A bit sunburned, but relaxed by a day at the ocean."

"Good. The island is working her magic."

The two were silent a long time as they admired Clark's work. Finally Hazy spoke.

"Do you have time to listen to a story?"

"A story? About what?"

"Just a fable. I feel expansive," she replied lightly.

"A story." This interesting woman always caught her off guard. Turning, she decided she'd better escape. "Have you seen Mander? We've gotten separated."

Hazy stared at her, then took a deep swallow of her amber drink. "The last I saw of her, she was watching a tennis match on the telly with a bunch of her buddies. She shan't miss you."

"All right then, let's have your story." She studied Hazy,

noting that she was dressed neatly in a white boatneck shell and white cotton trousers. White canvas deck shoes covered her feet. She was beautiful, seeming to glow against the backdrop of the evening.

"Not here, too many people, let's move outside."

Hazy led the way and they slipped through a nearby door onto the outer deck. That too was crowded with earnestly talking people so Hazy impatiently took her hand and led her along the side and across the gangway off the boat.

Moving along the dock where the houseboat was tied, Nina began to worry. They were going awfully far from Clark's boat. As she was about to speak up, Hazy stopped abruptly and led her down another gangway onto a silent, darkened cruiser.

"Hazy, what are…"

"One moment, just tryin' to get the lantern lit. There."

A soft glow filled the fore cabin and Nina could see Hazy outlined against the light as she came toward her.

"Whose boat is this? Are we trespassing?" Nina asked looking about nervously.

"Oh no, I know the owner. It's all right." Hazy led her into the cabin.

Anxiety filled Nina. She felt thrust into some surrealistic drawing where everything was shaded, obscure. Like Aaron's painting. She wanted to pull back and refuse to enter the cabin, but felt helpless, desire for this strange, magnetic woman engulfing her.

There was a double bed recessed in one side of the small, neat room and the sight of it alarmed Nina. She knew, with an awful certainty, that Hazy would have to do very little coaxing to get her there.

As if sensing her alarm, Hazy drew two captain's chairs together from opposite ends of the room. She positioned them back to back and, with an open hand, welcomed Nina into one.

Nina moved forward cautiously and lowered herself into the chair on her right.

Hazy moved around and sat facing away from her in the other chair.

"Hazy? Why are we sitting this way?"

Hazy sighed deeply. "So I can talk to you with a semblance of sanity."

"What?"

"Never mind. Just listen to me, please?" The pleading note in her voice silenced Nina.

After a brief moment of quiet, her low voice broke the night.

"Once upon a time there was a little duck. This duck grew up in very happy surroundings, floating on the marsh with his brother and sister ducks. Even though hunters roamed the marsh, the little duck felt very secure in the bosom of his family.

"Then one day the duck spied a cute little lady duck. He was very attracted to her, but knew they could never find love because the lady duck was from a very important duck family and her feathers were very white and her beak very orange.

"The little duck, who was from the mallard family, knew he could never be good enough for the lady duck because his feathers were too dull and his beak too muddy. But it was all right. The duck had his family and he knew love would find him someday.

"Then the fine lady duck finally noticed the little dark duck and began to spend time with him. The duck was ecstatic and soon did not pay attention to what he truly felt and believed because he was so swept up in the love and relationship. He couldn't see the warning signs.

"After the lady duck had made her duck family angry by being with the little dark duck, and after she had totally destroyed the dark duck's life and emotions, she flew away and went to live with another fine duck on the bay where the duckweed grows greenest."

Nina sighed, deeply saddened by the tale. "Oh, Hazy, so tragic! Why are you telling me this sad story?"

"Shhh, just listen. I need you to listen to me."

Nina settled back, her bare shoulders pressing against the soft cotton of Hazy's shirt.

"The little duck was, of course, devastated. He moped about for weeks blaming himself. He was short with the members of his family and snapped at the few friends who came to visit.

"One bright sunny day, after the duck had argued with his brother and his mother and father duck, he heard this horrible roar that echoed across the marsh. Investigating, he discovered mother and father duck had been killed by hunters."

Involuntarily, Nina gasped.

"The family scattered then, all the children coping with their pain and loss, and the little duck, realizing the world was no longer a safe haven, withdrew from everything he had valued before.

"He concentrated on building things and supplying things that other ducks needed even while he mocked these other ducks for needing these things. What did he need with these things? He had no life.

"He did very well, but was never happy again. Then one day, after many years had passed—"

A sudden call outside the boat broke off Hazy's story and Mander's voice calling for Nina carried clearly to them.

"Hell and damnation!" Hazy rose and dimmed the lantern. She turned to study Nina's face in the dimness, then swept her up from the chair and into her arms. Hazy's lips captured Nina in a deep kiss that made her legs go weak and planes of crystal pleasure rebound throughout her body. Her arms crept up and pulled Hazy's head closer, meshing them until she felt the world drop away.

Finally, Hazy seemed to find the strength to pull away, her breathing ragged, and she pushed Nina toward the door.

"Go now. Act like you were exploring the boats." Her voice was harsh and low.

"But—"

"Go, I said!"

Nina turned back and her eyes met Hazy's. She saw pain and an incredible longing there and it surprised her. She almost rushed back to hold her, would have if Hazy hadn't extinguished the lantern, leaving them in darkness. Gingerly, she felt her way out of the cabin and onto the deck. The harbor lights helped her find her way off the vessel and she raced toward Aaron's houseboat.

Chapter 23

Nina didn't see Hazy at all the next morning. She did see Mama New and Heather though, as they worked cleaning the graveled grounds around the cottages.

As their laughing voices carried through the window where she sat trying to work at the kitchen table, she descended easily into the depths of nagging guilt. How could she let herself feel so much for another woman's partner?

Extramarital affairs were something she did not approve of and not just from a moral standpoint. People always ended up hurt. Seeking sex and companionship outside the relationship only bred trouble. Divorce, part or work it out, Nina believed. Then search out a new companion.

Her overwhelming attraction to Hazy had definitely given her more insight into this particular dilemma and she knew she would never again judge a situation concerning infidelity unless she heard the extenuating circumstances first.

Why was she falling in love with Hazy? It was a force she could not control or deny, sweeping over her and wrecking her peace of mind. There was some quality about Hazy, something unseen and only sensed, that made her realize this was her companion, the woman she was supposed to be with. And that kiss…those kisses…

Nina simply could not think about them.

Hazy was taken, not for Nina to have.

And Mama New was such a sweet woman. This rankled even more.

Rising and pacing about the cottage, Nina grabbed her head between her two hands. What was she to do? Her mind kept hearing Hazy's smooth accented voice as she told her the duck story. The duck story—now what exactly did that mean? From the way Hazy had set up the telling of the story it had urgent importance to her and it was tragic that it had been interrupted by Mander.

And the kiss on the boat. It was better not to think about that kiss. The passion of that kiss had made all the other kisses she had received in her short life pale into insignificance.

She kept seeing Hazy's face just before she turned off the lantern in the cabin of the boat. What were her thoughts then? She had sensed great frustration and need. How did Hazy really feel toward her? Maybe she did have feelings for Nina. Maybe, just maybe, she and Mama New had a bad relationship. Maybe they were even contemplating a breakup. *Stop it, Nina!* she scolded herself.

Heather's piping voice, lifted in song, wafted to her and she suddenly felt trapped.

Maybe all this was just wishful thinking. She wondered what she would do if Hazy came to her a free woman. Or what if she came to her and swept her into a physical and emotional relationship while still involved with Mama New?

She fiddled with the cartridge pen lying on the Formica tabletop. Hazy could actually do it, dragging a willing Nina with her, and this scared the daylights out of her.

Frustrated and unable to keep still, she moved to peer out the screen door. Mama New was on her knees in a small patch of grass next to one of the rental cottages. With gentle, dust-smudged hands, she was trying to coax a weary marigold into standing upright. She finally found a small crooked twig and, pushing it into the ground next to the flower heads, wrapped the leaves of the flower around it for support. Rising from her crouched position, she arched her back with both hands and caught sight of Nina out of the corner of her eye. She waved cheerfully and Nina waved back.

Moving away from the door, Nina turned and pressed her back into the paneled wall of her cottage. How could she even think these thoughts? What kind of a woman was she? What kind of woman was that blasted Hazy Duncan?

Chapter 24

Emma Loreli was a very tall, very thin woman and she towered over Nina as she welcomed her with a bear hug. Heavy winds, laden with salt, had given her skin a weathered ruggedness but her smile was still youthful as she pulled back to grin at her visitor.

"So tell me the news. How is your ma?"

Nina shrugged. "I haven't seen her in a week now, although Dad called the other day. He says she's doing fine."

"And your da?" Mrs. Loreli asked, her head tilted to one side.

"He's fine. He sent me a new book." Nina's eyes were darting around Mrs. Loreli's small trailer, avoiding the older woman's penetrating gaze.

"All right, all right," Mrs. Loreli said firmly as she pulled Nina to the scarred kitchen table. "Sit here a minute."

Nina sat anxiously as Mrs. Loreli systematically filled the silver teakettle with water, placed it onto a lit gas burner, and prepared two cups with tea bags. The silence between them was companionable and Nina watched gulls scrabble on the ground outside the window.

Soon the two women had steaming cups of tea before them and a plate of homemade cookies to share.

"Now, tell me what's troubling you."

Nina smiled sheepishly, "It's nothing. Really."

"It's got to be something. I've never seen you mope so. You look like a fisherman who just lost a whole net of tuna." She leaned forward, and using a ploy Nina remembered from when she was a young girl, caught Nina's eyes and said very seriously, "You better tell old lady Loreli."

"It's just a little trouble," Nina said with a laugh.

"So what's Mander done to you? She always was an impetuous girl."

Nina's head snapped up. "How do you know about Mander?"

Mrs. Loreli baptized Nina with a secretive wink. "This is a small island, love, everybody knows everything. Someone saw the two of you together at Duffy's and it's not hard to put two and two together. Or in this case, one and one."

Nina didn't answer for a long while and the two sipped their tea.

"You know the woman who runs Channel Haven?" Nina asked finally.

"Sure, Hazel. Hazel Duncan," Mrs. Loreli answered eyeing Nina curiously.

"What about her? She's with Mama New, right?" She hung her head, embarrassed to have asked the question.

"Now there's a sad tale," Mrs. Loreli said, reaching for a cookie.

Nina looked up. "How so? You mean Hazy's family?"

"Mama New. Well, and Hazy, too."

The younger woman squirmed with curiosity. "Tell me about it."

Mrs. Loreli chuckled. "You never could resist a good story,

even when you were ten years old and out here visiting Tom for the summer." A wave of sadness washed across her features as she mentioned Nina's grandfather.

Nina laid a comforting hand along Mrs. Loreli's forearm. "You really do miss him, don't you? I do too."

Mrs. Loreli stared out the window, her eyes dreamy and unfocused. "He was my life for so long. Now that he's gone, I feel empty."

"Me too," Nina replied. "I thought I saw him the other day, standing on the porch of the house."

"I see him in my garden, where he used to stand gazing out over Little Oyster Bay," the older woman confided with a fond smile.

"Why did you two never marry?" Nina asked hesitantly, hoping Mrs. Loreli wouldn't take offense at the prying.

Mrs. Loreli shrugged. "We didn't feel the need. We were happy."

She abruptly straightened her back. "Now, enough of that foolishness. About Mama New. Her husband was Seth Newcomb, who everyone called Newt because he was so quick to scamper up the mainsail, and he was like a brother to Hazel and her brothers and sisters. The group of them played cards every Friday night, come hell or high water. Except when one or the other was at sea, of course. Seth worked as a commercial fisherman on the *Roving Eye*.

"Then one fall, when they were starting out the season, he was killed trying to loosen a net snare near the main ship. He went into the water to get a better hold and the waves snapped his craft around and crushed him between the two boats."

She sighed and continued. "It damn near killed everybody else too. Mama New almost lost her mind, the grief was so great. Hazy suffered mightily. There was nothing anybody could do though, except give him the best funeral possible and get on with life. Hazy has been living with Mama New ever since."

"But are they together? Like, you know…" Nina persisted.

Was there a chance they weren't involved?

Mrs. Loreli eyed Nina with certainty. "Of course. How could they not be together that way? There's something mighty going on between the two. People have been speculating about it since before Newt's death and some even said if he'd had his mind on his work that day and not on what might have been happenin' at home, he might never have gotten himself killed." She nodded her head emphatically. "Besides, I've never seen Hazy turn down a pretty skirt."

"Oh no, I thought so," Nina murmured with a deep sigh.

"See here, you've not got designs on Hazy now, do you?"

Nina studied Mrs. Loreli. "Why? I just thought…"

"Well, don' ye think no more about it."

Mrs. Loreli rose and paced to the kitchen sink to rinse out her cup. Her movements were angry. "I've seen the people hurt by that woman. She's a devil, I tell you. The youngest Grenier gull was led astray by Hazy. Oh, the stories she'd tell about Hazy's anger and abuse. Her parents finally sent her to the mainland and she's married to a nice young man now, doing well."

"She can be an ogre," Nina agreed sadly, "I've seen that firsthand."

"Well, mark my words, young woman, I warned ye. Watch out for her. She's too much a man by half, crashing in an' takin' what she wants, then movin' on, with nary a look back."

She studied Nina, amusement entering her eyes. "Feel better? I sure can cheer it up now, can't I?" Her laughter was warm and deep.

Nina allowed a small smile. "Yeah, I feel a lot better," she said sarcastically.

"Well, come on out here in back and get your mind off what's troublin' you." Mrs. Loreli beckoned, holding the screen door open invitingly. "I don't know why none of the young island women won't appeal to you, like Mander there. You've such a beauty about you and can have any of them, I'm sure."

They walked around to the back of Mrs. Loreli's trailer and

into the lovely garden she had designed and planted there. Large, strangely luxuriant scrub pines shaded the area and provided a separated alcove from the bay that reached within several feet of Mrs. Loreli's home. And though the water could only be glimpsed briefly through foliage, the gentle slap of the water carried easily to them.

Mrs. Loreli bent and swiped viciously at her calf. "Darned bugs, they love ta heat."

"Why have you never moved from the island?" asked Nina, her voice pensive. She was propped atop a rock wall on the far side of the garden.

"Move from the island?" Her tone was one of incredulity. "Why would I want to do that?"

Nina shrugged. "Oh, I don't know. To escape the insects, the hurricanes, the isolation."

"Why, Nina Christie! Tom must be rolling in his grave. We both thought you had the island in you, else he never woulda left the house with you."

Nina felt chastened. "I'm sorry. I was just curious about your life. I understand why you love it here, I do too. Really."

Mrs. Loreli studied Nina with arms folded across her chest. "You are in a rotten place today, aren't you? About my life, it's nothing too glorious. You know most of the story. I came ta the island from the shore as Chester Loreli's wife back in 'fifty-two. We bought this land here when land was still agoing dirt-cheap and started buildin' rental houses. We was lucky too, you know, because we got in right on the crest of the tourism wave. There were still a lot of ponies then, and the pony penning had only been held a couple of times regular. We did well, able to make a livin' without Chester having to go out on the boats."

She paused and deftly pruned pale leaves from a lush myrtle bush. "I never felt any urge to leave, even after my Chester died. The island is my home and I have the trailer here till the day I die," she finished. She turned to Nina. "It's your home now too, you know."

Nina stared out at the bay. "Yes, and I'm glad."

Mrs. Loreli nodded curtly. "Good then. And don't let the tourists get to you. They come in like a lion but they peter out like a lamb. They come and they go. A good way to mark time." She chuckled as if admiring her wit.

Later, as the two women walked along Little Oyster Bay, Mrs. Loreli shared the history of the islands with Nina, much as she had done when Nina was a child and they had walked with Grandpapa Tom. They speculated on pirate's treasure. Mrs. Loreli held a firm conviction there was still much gold buried on Assateague Island while Nina pooh-poohed the idea.

Another point of contention was the ponies; Mrs. Loreli said pirates brought them, while Nina held that the Indians rescued them from an English ship. Neither believed they were of Spanish stock as the brochures allowed.

When the sun's shadows lengthened across the bay, Nina took her leave of Emma Loreli and headed for Main Street. She browsed for some time in various clothing and souvenir shops, finally purchasing a wind chime for her new house and a new pair of silvered sunglasses.

She tried very hard *not* to think of Hazy. She almost succeeded.

Chapter 25

Hazy was in the living room of cottage eight when Nina returned to Channel Haven later that evening. She sat on one end of the sofa, one bare foot on the floor and one on the sofa cushion. Her hand, holding a smoldering cigarette, dangled from the upraised knee.

She seemed oblivious to the rapidly darkening room so Nina crossed to the light switch and turned on the overhead light. Only then did Hazy look up at her.

"You forgot to lock your door," she said softly.

"And you decided to come in and make yourself at home?" Nina wasn't fond of having her privacy invaded and her voice displayed this fact.

"Just protecting my livelihood. You get ripped off, I get ripped off." She took a deep drag from the cigarette, the red tip blooming into new life.

"Well, thanks," Nina murmured. She glanced to the desk to

verify her computer was still there.

She moved into the bedroom and laid her bags on top of the bureau. Then she re-entered the living room and studied Hazy doubtfully.

"I didn't know you smoked," she said as she crossed to the refrigerator.

"Don't," Hazy replied, her tone curt. "Just felt the need for one."

"I don't have beer, will soda do?" Nina asked returning with two cans.

At Hazy's nod, she handed her one, then pulled a chair from the kitchen table and sat facing her.

Out of the corner of her eye, Nina caught a glimpse of an extraordinarily beautiful sunset glowing behind the picture window. "Would you look at that," she sighed. "That red-orange is an incredible color. I'm glad my grandfather lived on Chincoteague. I can't think of a better place to live."

"When will the house be ready?" Hazy asked, crushing her cigarette in the ashtray she had placed on the windowsill.

Nina watched as Hazy took a deep swallow of the soda. She loved the clean line of her jaw. "Mander talks like it'll be complete before the end of next week. My folks are bringing my furniture out next weekend so I hope to move in officially then. Who told you about the house?"

"No one, and everyone. It's a small island, if one person knows, everyone knows."

A silence fell then. Nina watched the sunset.

Hazy placed the canned soda on the windowsill next to the sofa and let her foot drop to the floor.

"Come here," she said softly.

Nina turned wide eyes her way. "What?"

"Come here."

She motioned Nina over with a sideways nod of her head.

Nina retreated, a little frightened. "Why? What do you want?"

Hazy sat forward, resting her elbows on her knees. "I want you, Nina, because you're driving me crazy. I can't stop thinking about you, imagining what it would be like to...just come here." She extended a hand.

Nina was confused. She wanted, with her whole being, to fly into her arms and let Hazy fan the fire that was suddenly suffusing her body, but this desire frightened her. She'd never been so consumed. It was daunting.

Hazy stood and moved sensuously, like a panther, toward Nina. Gaining Nina's side, she leaned back and pressed a palm to the side of Nina's neck and jaw, under her long hair. The smell of the cigarette on her was somehow sexy and Nina inhaled deeply as her eyes closed.

The sensation of the hand against the tender skin there almost made Nina stop breathing. The hand was hot, strong and callused. Nina felt surrounded by seawater, from the scent and the power of Hazy.

"Don't you want me, Nina?" she whispered as she came closer, falling to her knees and pushing the trunk of her body between Nina's unresisting thighs. "Don't you want me the way I want you?"

She pressed her lips to the left of Nina's breastbone, above where the frantically beating heart moved the fabric of her shirt. The electric shock made Nina gasp aloud.

With irresistible force, her arms came up and curved around Hazy's neck and shoulders. She cradled the platinum-blond head against her body.

Hazy sighed, as if in relief, and laid hot, soft lips upon the thin skin of Nina's neck above her collarbone as she brought her hand down and smoothed its warmth along Nina's bare arm.

"Why do you make me feel this way?" she asked, lips and breath tickling and raising delicious gooseflesh. "It's na fair to stir a woman so, to invade her mind until she can think of little else but how it would feel to touch you this way."

Hazy drew back to cup Nina's face in her hands. Her lips

captured Nina and Nina felt momentarily dizzy from the possession. The kiss was invasive, but never taking more than was offered, merely coaxing Nina along until she responded with a passion that surprised with its intensity.

Hazy kissed Nina's eyes, one at a time; moist, lingering kisses.

"Tell me you want me, Nina," she whispered hoarsely. "You do, don't you?"

Her hands dropped to stroke Nina's breasts through her thin shirt and undershirt. Fire leapt throughout Nina's body and her face felt flushed and warm.

"Yes, yes, I do," she whispered, wanting to whimper from the ecstasy of Hazy's touch.

Everything was forgotten—Mama New, Heather, her parents, even Mrs. Loreli's warning; all were blazed away in this molten core of heat. She was lost, not knowing where—or who— she was. The world was vanishing except for Hazy, herself and the hot cocoon of sensation surrounding them.

Hazy hesitantly lifted the bottom hem of her shirt, as if asking permission. In answer, Nina lifted her arms. Hazy drew both shirts off and, with a sigh, proceeded to worship Nina's upper body with lips and rough, hot palms.

When Nina was pliant, swaying in the chair from kisses and caresses, Hazy stood. With impatient passion, she snapped off the overhead light and turned to lift Nina to her feet and propel her through the twilight into the bedroom. She pressed against her as she slowly, fully undressed them both, the last shards of sunlight making her golden hair shimmer.

When they lay next to one another on the bed, Nina rose above Hazy and cupped her lean breasts, teasing the small hard nipples into a puckered firmness with lips and hands until she brought helpless moans to Hazy's lips. Nina touched the thick blond hair, finally allowed, then looked deep into the cobalt of her eyes trying to understand so much.

Hazy took over, welcoming Nina into an embrace. Hazy began to love her, gently, patiently, but urgently. Somehow, even with the aching necessity rampant in both of them, Hazy managed to take the time to discover exactly what pleased Nina and what sent her to the brink of ecstatic insanity.

"I think you do want me as much as I have to…have you," she gasped once as Nina's hand insistently closed on the softest part of her as they pressed together with eagerness.

Nina smiled to herself in the dimness. Oh yes, she wanted Hazy. More than she'd ever wanted anyone.

Hazy moved down and pressed her warm mouth against the tender spot below Nina's navel, the sensation forcing Nina to bite her bottom lip to keep from crying out.

"Ah, Nina, I care for you too much, too much," Hazy murmured against her yielding flesh as she moved lower, her mouth powerful against Nina's clit. Rocked by the fierce current of passion wrought by each stroke of Hazy's tongue, within moments Nina felt new wetness as she cried out her release. Hazy entered her then, gently, fulfilling and completing the orgasm. Closing her eyes Hazy pressed her forehead against Nina's thigh as if savoring the waning pulsations of Nina's body.

After some time Hazy looked up at her and Nina was surprised to see moisture shining in the shadowed eyes when the lighthouse made its brief survey across the room. A great surge of fear welled in her. She needed to tell Hazy to go, needed to escape this frightening need that consumed her. And then there was the foreignness of the new tenderness she felt for the gruff, stiff woman. She was seeing the real Hazy and the thought filled her with a fierce protectiveness.

Nina pulled Hazy close and rained soft kisses along her neck, her jaw, soft warm tongue pressing designs. Hazy countered by roughly teasing one firm breast peak with the tip of her fingers. Renewed reaction made Nina powerless and she threw back her head, flashing currents of pure pleasure shooting from breast to crotch. Breathless, she pulled Hazy closer, her fingers fluttering along the other's back like butterflies at nectar.

Murmuring, Hazy moved to embrace her and their bodies

slid together. Both gasped and stilled as they made the full connection of heated, wet flesh against thighs. Nina marveled at the new physical awareness she felt coursing through her. The thought, *I've found it*, played repeatedly through her mind, like a welcome melody.

Hazy spoke as her body trembled, her face buried in the curve of Nina's neck. "Please," she beseeched in a harsh whisper. "Please."

They lay clasped together, Nina driven to the brink of madness by wanting, by fear. She moved then, slowly and sweetly, ocean waves against the shore. Nina's hands found Hazy's waist and muscular bottom, encouraging her as they met and kissed with every slow push. Hazy's right hand went low and drove Nina momentarily insane as her kisses plundered her mouth, furthering the sensation and taking Nina from her body with each forceful thrust of hot fingers within her. She faded away into another dimension as Hazy shuddered against her with muted cries.

The whispers against her mouth were low and enticing, bringing Nina back to reality. Hazy's words of endearment were incomprehensible but increased Nina's fire anew. Driven by unnamed need, she rolled Hazy onto her back and lay atop her. Hazy's wet hands moved along her flanks, raising gooseflesh. Nina smoothed the hair from Hazy's eyes, finding them sweet and vulnerable yet still darkened with desire.

The unhurried tenderness juxtaposed with fierce need touched her heart as well as her body and the flames seared her far more deeply than any mere physical encounter.

Nina knew she was hopelessly hooked. She would, unfortunately, love Hazy Duncan forever.

Chapter 26

The gulls woke Hazy at daybreak the next morning. Nina still slumbered in the crook of her arm. Impulsively, she touched her lips to her forehead, inhaling the clean, sweet scent of her hair.

The passion they had created the night before lingered and Hazy felt aroused and satisfied at the same time. She smiled at the ceiling as she remembered Nina's intensity. At last she'd found a woman who matched her, a woman whose passion was as strong as her own.

Or had she? There was still Mander to contend with. She was, by far, the better catch—younger, stronger, more socially desirable. Would Nina choose Mander over a mere boat jockey who was more than two decades older?

If she had any sense she would.

Hazy eased her arm from beneath Nina and held her breath as the other woman stirred and turned over, drawing up her knees.

Hazy left the bed gingerly and drew the blanket up to cover Nina.

After gathering her clothes and moving into the living room, she dressed as she gazed out at the channel through the screen door.

She loved mornings. The world was stirring, waking with a special magic right before her eyes. There was so much to see and each sunrise was a new uplifting experience. She realized suddenly that every time she was with Nina she felt the same way, even during their petty arguments. She made her feel like each day was a new start on life.

Nina. Hazy sighed and pressed her forehead into the nylon screen.

What was she going to do now? Head over heels in love and she'd sworn she'd have no more of that.

Smiling at her stubbornness, she knew she should have realized her self-destructive personality wouldn't be warned off by sticking her hand in the fire. Oh no, it only made her want to jump into the fire headfirst. She just *had* to wait for Nina in the cottage. She couldn't leave her a note about the door left unlocked; it had to be told face to face.

Well, now it was done and she knew the right thing to do.

To love again and lose again would destroy what little that was left of her. Yet she was taking the chance because of Nina and that special way she made her feel, as if every day were filled with mornings.

A car passing reminded her she had work to do. The usual morning rush of rental customers would be arriving soon and it wouldn't do for them, or Mama New, to see her coming from Nina's cottage.

She slipped out the door, closing it quietly.

Chapter 27

Nina woke feeling as though her body had been reborn. Her skin tingled and she couldn't remember a time she'd felt so deliciously relaxed. Memories flooded her mind and, blushing, she relived the night before.

Hazel loved her, she was sure of it. Love was a hard emotion to define, but she had seen it shining in Hazy's eyes as she let down her guard. Every action had generated tenderness and caring. And how could someone consistently imitate those feelings? How could she lie to her during the special intimacy they had shared? Hazy had transported her to a world of pure sensation and warmth where both had forgotten everything except the radiant love shining between them.

But where was Hazy? Why wasn't she here with her? Her heart fell. She was with her family, of course. Nina didn't even hear the usual morning activity. Occasional snatches of conversation reached her from the other cottages, a television blared somewhere, and a boat engine rumbled to life, that was all.

She sat up abruptly in the bed, her tousled hair falling across her face in a fiery, auburn wave. What if she already regretted last night? Suppose she was eaten up with guilt because of Mama New and Heather? Did she hate her now for allowing her to betray her family? She stumbled out of bed.

After showering and dressing in simple shorts and T-shirt, Nina paced the cottage in a nervous frenzy. Why wouldn't Hazy come to her?

Thoroughly distracted by worry and uncontrolled curiosity, Nina decided she'd have to go to Hazy.

Clothes flapping on a clothesline outside Hazy's cottage made her pause halfway across the drive and reconsider everything that had been happening to her. The clothes were of an intimate nature—bras, panties, a slip or two—and several large flowered dresses that could only belong to Mama New. Interspersed with these hung Hazy's shorts and T-shirts, as well as small colorful dresses and lace-edged panties, no doubt belonging to a precious child named Heather.

Dismay swamped Nina. What was she doing? Did she really think Hazy could have a life with her?

They did love one another, she told herself, and these things were known to happen every day. But to continue to betray Mama New? That kind, sweet woman?

Even if Hazy and Mama New weren't committed to one another, Nina was interfering in some type of long-term relationship and it just wasn't right. Filled with sorrow and guilt, Nina quickly returned to her cottage and the safety of solitude.

Nevertheless, some hours later, when a knock sounded at door, her heart leapt with sudden joy. Nina quickly checked her appearance in the bedroom mirror then raced to the door.

Rhonda stood outside the screen, a large bouquet of flowers clasped to her chest.

Chapter 28

Glancing past Rhonda, Nina saw Hazy standing in the drive. She was talking to Martha Jennings. Hazy caught Nina's eye. Her expression was bewildered but cool.

"Well, I knew my greeting would be cold, but I didn't think it would be nonexistent." Rhonda's statement drew her attention and Nina stared numbly into dark gray eyes.

She had forgotten how well-groomed Rhonda kept herself. People on the island lived more close to nature. Gray hair and casual clothing were the norm. Rhonda was certainly more metropolitan; her hair was impeccable, her flawless skin smoothly oiled and bearing just the right amount of tan. She wore designer clothing and a silk scarf decorated the front of her button-down shirt. Her leather loafers, even in ruthless August heat, held a hard-won gleam.

"Well, please say something, or at least let me come inside." She looked from side to side. "It's embarrassing to be kept waiting on your doorstep."

Nina found her voice finally. "Rhonda, you're here."

"Yes, I am. May I come in?" She was frowning and Nina knew from experience that she was becoming angry. Renewed anger filled Nina. As if Rhonda had any right to be angry.

Opening the door, Nina curtly stepped aside so Rhonda could enter. Rhonda paused as she passed and Nina thought for a minute that she was actually going to kiss her. She braced to push her away. She passed on, however, and laid the flowers on the kitchen table.

"I brought these for you. A way of apologizing, I suppose," she said in a low voice, her back to Nina. "Although I don't suppose anything can make up for what happened."

Nina was finally recovering from the shock of Rhonda's return and a wealth of hard memories flooded her. She felt her own anger soar.

"Flowers? You brought me flowers? Are these supposed to make me feel better?" she snapped in fury as she turned to face Rhonda.

"I really am sorry for what I've put you through," Rhonda said softly. "I just got cold feet, I suppose. I went back to Wendy. That's where I've been." She hung her head.

Nina turned away from Rhonda and covered her face with her hands. She'd left her for Wendy? Wendy was her high school sweetheart and they had broken up years ago. Or so Rhonda claimed.

"I thought it was over between you two. You weren't still seeing her when you were with me, were you?" She turned and eyed Rhonda with anger and pain.

"No, not really," she answered quickly. "She would call me now and then, but that's all."

"Then why?" Nina grated. "Why did you go to her and why did you bother to ask me to be your life partner? Why did you not even have the simple decency to tell me what was going on with you?"

Rhonda walked to the bedroom doorway and leaned against the jamb, arms crossed. "I wanted you, Nina, still do. I just had to make sure what I had with Wendy was really over." She sighed. "And...I was afraid of a real commitment."

"Oh, hell. We talked and talked about that," Nina reminded her. "You're a liar! You said you were okay with committing."

Rhonda held up her hands. "I just realized I couldn't face all those people at that party, and..." she paused and raised sheepish eyes. "I just ran."

Nina nodded. "Yes. You just ran," she snarled. "Leaving me with friends and relatives wanting to know where you were, with the ceremony to cancel, dresses to return. You can't imagine the hell I went through. The embarrassment."

"I know, I'm sorry, I just..."

Hazy and Martha entered the cottage, Martha laughing at some witticism Hazy had shared with her, and it worked to help dispel the tension filling the small room.

Upon seeing Nina, Martha rushed across the room to fling silk-covered arms about her neck. "Nina, Nina, how are you, sweet girl?"

"Hello, Martha," Nina said politely, trying to smile. Circumstances made it hard to show the excitement she normally would have shown.

"I hope you don't mind my bringing Rhonda along. I was visiting with your parents when she showed up looking for you. I had planned to visit and thought she might as well come along."

"Yes, that's fine," Nina replied quickly, trying to put Martha at ease. "We have some things that need to be sorted out anyway."

Hazy was watching the exchange with curiosity. Nina saw her eye the flowers lying on the table so she moved to unwrap them and put them in a vase of water.

Martha, Hazy and Rhonda stood in awkward silence until Rhonda spoke to Hazy.

"Must be quite a business you have here, with the influx of tourists each year," she said with a polished, friendly smile. "Does it go on all year long or is it seasonal only?"

"Well, actually," Hazy began, boldly moving to take a seat at the table, as if laying claim. "It goes on pretty much all year 'round now. Used to be just during the pony penning or oyster season. Now it seems like people have realized how nice the islands are all year long. I do business up until way after first freeze."

"Do you do the cottages as well as boats?" Rhonda asked, joining Hazy and audaciously miming for Nina to bring them both a drink.

Nina looked at her in disbelief. Shaking her head, she fetched a pitcher of iced tea from the refrigerator and glasses from the cupboard. She poured two glasses over on the counter then placed the pitcher and two empty glasses on the table with a thud.

Chapter 29

While Hazy and Rhonda served their own tea and discussed the tourist business, Martha and Nina escaped to the boat rental dock with their glasses of cool, sweet tea and settled themselves on the two end Adirondack chairs.

"How are you, really," Martha asked brushing Nina's hair from her face so she could see the younger woman's eyes. "Was bringing Rhonda a no-no?"

"You might have given me a heads-up," she retorted then shrugged and looked out toward the channel. "No, I need to resolve things with her."

"Did you find out what happened? I only made small talk with her on the drive over. I didn't want her to think I was prying."

"Well," Nina sighed. "She says she got cold feet." She couldn't bring herself to tell Martha that she went back to her old girlfriend.

Martha nodded wisely. "It's happened before. So, why is she

back?"

"That I don't know yet," she replied firmly. "But I intend to find out."

"Well, don't do it right now," Martha suggested. "I've made lunch reservations for the three of us at The Elite. Do you think your nice friend Hazy would like to join us?"

"No," Nina snapped, startling her friend so much that she almost spilled tea from the glass she was raising to her lips. "I'm sure she has work to do."

She knew her nerves would not be able to stand Hazy and Rhonda in the same space for long. Rhonda's sudden appearance confused her. And being near Hazy still made her skin tingle and overwhelmed her with desire.

Martha eyed Nina's pink cheeks as if wondering what her thoughts could be. "Well, if you're sure."

"Sure," Nina said firmly. "Listen, why don't you go fetch my bag for me. It's just inside the bedroom door. I think I'll wait here."

She handed her empty glass to a puzzled Martha, then walked over to stand by Martha's car.

Hazy came out a moment later and her questioning blue eyes captured Nina.

Nina wanted to rush to her, to kiss her, to wrap her in her arms. But the best thing for both of them was for Nina to stay as far away from Hazy as possible.

Martha came up behind her then and Hazy turned away. Nina took her bag from Martha.

"Hazy," Nina called and walked to her.

She could smell the wonderful open-air scent that seemed so much a part of her, could feel the heat radiating from her sun-bronzed skin and had to fight the urge to nibble at her neck where a slow pulse throbbed.

"Nina," she said gently. "Are you okay?"

"Yes, I think so," Nina answered timidly.

"What's goin' on," she asked, nodding to indicate Martha and

Rhonda.

Tears filled Nina's eyes and she could only shake her head. Why couldn't life be simpler?

Conscious that Rhonda and Martha were watching her every move, Nina reached into her handbag and counted out the money she owed Channel Haven for her second week.

"Here, here's what I owe you for next week's rental," she said.

She felt rather than saw Hazy's back stiffen at her words. "What are ye tryin' to prove, Nina?"

"Please Hazy, just take the money," she pleaded, her voice catching on a sob. "This is business."

Anger transformed Hazy's features as she roughly grasped Nina's upper arm and turned her so her back was to the other two women.

She released Nina, jerked the money from her hand then stuffed it helter-skelter back into the handbag. "I da na need your mainland payoff nor none of your pitiful excuses," she growled, her accent growing thick from anger. "Be off with ye're friends and lovers. I shan't sit about and mewl after you, ye can be assured of that."

She stomped toward the office and Nina, heart heavy, walked slowly toward Martha's car. Heartbroken, she nevertheless felt certain keeping Hazy at a distance was the best thing to do.

Chapter 30

Lunch proved pleasant even though Nina's heart throbbed low in her chest like a worn engine.

Martha and Rhonda carried most of the conversation, eating heartily of the fresh seafood delicacies offered by one of the island's finest restaurants. Nina answered when spoken to and picked at the food. She saw Martha watching her with a worried frown and tried to push away the gloom engulfing her. She joined into a conversation about the many types of gulls as her mind wondered what to do about Rhonda now that she was here. Obviously Rhonda wanted to resume their relationship as if nothing had happened.

Even if they could go on as before, she could definitely not trust her anymore; that much she knew for sure. How could she give her life and love to someone she couldn't trust implicitly?

Yes, she would definitely send Rhonda away and continue alone, praying no one found out about the madness between her and Hazy. And madness was what it had been. A fast and furious infatuation, impossible to allow. She had been loved by Hazy and had loved her in return. Now she could move away at the end of the week and try to avoid her in the future. Perhaps someday they would meet by accident and could laugh about the strange chemistry that had thrown them together for that brief moment in time.

Nina swallowed hard, fervently hoping that day would never come. She didn't think she'd ever be able to face her alone without wanting her just as much as she had last night. As she did right now.

"So Nina, do you think you'll like living on the island?" Rhonda's voice was soft and intimate as she leaned across the table.

Martha had disappeared. Nina saw her enter the ladies' room.

"Yes, I already like it very much," Nina told her. "I can't wait for the house to be finished."

Rhonda watched her a moment then grasped her hand. "And us, Nina? What is our future? Do I have a chance? I know I live several hours away but I could relocate. My father has a blending company on the Eastern Shore and I'm sure he could transfer me there."

Though she had expected it, Nina was still appalled beyond belief. She was tired, so tired of this insane trend her life was taking. Her mind suddenly brightened and took an impulsive shift and she knew the right choice. She would avoid any relationships and live alone with her books, her music, and maybe a cat and some ducks for company.

She studied Rhonda with hard eyes, re-evaluating what life would have been like had she turned up for the commitment ceremony. What she had once considered a charmed existence no longer was the case. It was so obvious now: Rhonda was vain, spoiled, demanding and unpredictable. She hadn't even decently apologized for the hurt and humiliation she'd inflicted.

Then there was Hazy, who was quarrelsome, certainly a

womanizer, and betraying lovely Mama New.

Neither of them deserved her.

"Nina? Are you all right?" Rhonda was worried about her, she could see it in her long, sleek face. Nina's decision was made. "Yes, I'm fine, but we need to talk."

"Good," said Martha coming up behind her. "You can drop me off at my hotel so I can make some calls and you two can take my car and go for a nice long drive."

Rhonda protested politely but Martha insisted.

They left the restaurant and Martha drove to the Assateague Inn, where she passed the car to Nina and Rhonda.

From there they drove onto Assateague Island.

Most of the tourists had gone this late in the day but a few diehards were crabbing in the sun-heated backwater alongside the road. Rhonda drove all the way to the beach then turned and retraced their path until finally stopping at an overlook with a view of the salt marsh. The two of them sat silently for many moments.

"So, what do we need to talk about?" she said finally. "You're still mad about what I did—leaving you—aren't you?"

"No," Nina answered truthfully. "I don't think I am."

"Well, what is it then?"

Nina turned so she could see the other's face. "You and I have been seeing each other off and on since we were in college, right?"

"Actually, we started dating steadily after graduation," she corrected her, "but go on. This sounds like a real good Dear Jane letter. I guess I've got one coming."

Nina, angered by the remark, tried to remain calm. "Not exactly. I...I just think I've fallen out of love with you. I mean…" She paused as Rhonda sighed loudly and shifted in her seat. "No, really, I will always be your friend but I don't love you anymore."

"It's that Hazy woman, isn't it? That island bitch you're renting from. I saw the way she was looking at you. Are you sleeping with her?"

Nina's mouth fell open and her anger soared. "How dare you ask that? It's none of your business what I do now, not after what you did to me!"

"See? I knew you were still angry about that. You can't fool me."

She stared at her. Why shouldn't she be angry? She had every right. "I have no desire to fool you, Rhonda," she said heatedly. "For your information, Hazel Duncan is living with a wonderful woman and they are raising a family together. There's nothing between us."

She studied the smirking disbelief in Rhonda's face. "Look, just take me back to the cottage. I can see talking to you is a waste of time," she said finally. "This is a perfect example of why we can't maintain a relationship."

"No," Rhonda retorted. "We can't have a relationship because you obviously don't want one. With me anyway."

She started the car and they drove back to Channel Haven in silence.

Contrition stung her heart as she bid Rhonda a sad farewell. Knowing she would probably never see her again, she pensively took the ring from her wallet, handed it to her and kissed her cheek before getting out of the car. By that time the anger had almost dissipated, leaving only the sorrow that accompanies any failed relationship.

After Rhonda, stone-faced, pulled away from the Channel Haven parking lot, Nina immediately went toward the boat dock looking for Hazy. Not seeing her there, she walked across the landing to the small office. It was deserted.

Puzzled, as it was closing time for Hazy's boat rental business and she should have been nearby, Nina agonized over trying to find her. She knew she should stay far from her but just couldn't find it in herself to leave the anger simmering between them. Bravely, she crossed to Hazy's cottage behind the office and tapped gently on the door. She knocked harder. Still no answer.

Feeling a sense of desolation and loss she'd never felt before, Nina eased the screen door shut and staggered across the drive to her cottage, her eyes full of burning tears.

Chapter 31

Early the next morning, after a mostly sleepless night, Hazy climbed into her Jeep and drove to Assateague Beach.

She needed to lick her wounds and thought Assateague might be the place to do it. Who knew, maybe she'd find an adorable bikini-clad twit to help her forget about Nina.

She'd watched as Nina kissed Rhonda the night before and that pretty much told her old Hazy was out and fancy Rhonda in, and she was having a hard time deciding whether she was more hurt than angry or more angry than hurt.

Shifting gears with furious carelessness and goosing the Jeep up to reckless speeds through Assateague's quiet early morning peace, Hazy refused to be hurt by the woman's duplicity. Why should she let a mere woman destroy the peace she'd finally acquired in her life?

Hazy had waited for her to come back the night before, waited to apologize again for the way she'd treated her. She had actually felt sorry for Nina, actually sympathized with the position Rhonda's return left her in.

But she was wounded badly now, no denying it. She'd let down her guard too soon.

Well, she thought as she coasted a curve of road around the salt marsh, soon Nina would be safe in her little house with Rhonda and Hazy would never have to think of her again.

In fact, she had half a mind to go back and demand the money for the week's rental, sorry she had stuffed it back into her bag.

Hazy drove directly onto the beach at the far southern end and turned off the engine.

She sat ruminating for quite some time until the beach became more populated. She observed the people, seeking some visible clue as to how they found their happiness. There seemed no easy answer. Some couples walked by that were very close, touching and smiling at every opportunity. Others walked by who, though obviously together, were light years apart.

Hazy knew she was an intelligent woman. She was a natural born scholar—of books, and of life. She knew how fragile a relationship could be, how it required nurturing and tender care in order to survive. And this did not frighten her anymore. Though she had denied it for some time, thanks to her new feelings for Nina, she knew she was actually capable of nurturing a relationship. She also knew that she had finally found the right partner.

Yet what she had long feared about being involved with someone—that sharp scissor of betrayal that seemed to hover—had happened once again. Nina had betrayed her too.

A woman caught her eye. She was younger, but not by much, not as young as Nina, and she was wearing a white thong bikini that showed much of her deeply tanned skin. She walked by and smiled invitingly at Hazy.

After she passed, Hazy knew the woman would turn to make sure Hazy was watching. She did. Hazy also knew she would be miffed if she wasn't watching with appreciation. She was.

She could go after the woman and apologize for her

disinterest and could probably charm her way into the woman's arms but the effort seemed too great.

It seemed women were all the same. They needed the admiration of others to prove their worth. She'd thought Nina different.

Most women were interested in things she couldn't relate to, gossip and hairstyles and such nonsense. Not Nina. She knew books and her sharp, well-rounded mind could hold Hazy's interest easily.

Many women didn't like the idea of getting dirty, afraid to muss their hair or break a fingernail. Not Nina. She had even gone on a daring late-night swim in the channel with her and Hazy found herself admiring that bold, independent spirit.

Should she try to win her from Rhonda? She chewed her bottom lip and rubbed callused palms along her sun-warmed arms. Was the prize worth the fight? She thought of the night they'd spent together, a night of special, beautiful passion. Her mind roamed to their late-night swim and the way they had connected there in the water.

Then she remembered the first day she'd seen Nina, almost stepping on her in her haste to gain the office. Her first thought had been about how cute the freckles were that peppered Nina's pert nose and cheeks. Then Nina had giggled at her and she was on the way to being lost in love.

Tears filled her eyes but she made no move to wipe them away. And then there was Mama New and Heather. How could she explain all this to them? Uproot their lives? Would they understand this emotion that would take her away from them and have her with someone new? They certainly didn't understand her unusual behavior during the past few days.

Other women passed by throughout the morning but Hazy took no interest. Her thoughts were branded with the memory of Nina and she knew she loved her helplessly. But loved her recklessly, as well, for Nina obviously wanted to belong to another.

Chapter 32

Although Nina was sure she was doing the right thing, it didn't make her suffer any less.

In the morning, she woke and immediately thought of Hazy, aching to have her beside her, the heat of their bodies blending together.

She wondered occasionally who she was really saving—Mama New or herself? The feelings she carried for Hazy Duncan could easily consume, could take over her life. Maybe it was better to run now before she got any more involved and lost herself completely.

But the idea of being without Hazy was intolerable.

Life before Hazy—she had thought it full of meaning and vitality. Now she realized there had been only emptiness filled with duty to her parents and the happiness of the fictional lives portrayed in the books she read so avidly.

Facing that again was disheartening but she couldn't see

building a life together with Hazy either. They would always be at odds, especially with the memory of Mama New between them. We'd probably kill each other within the first week together anyway, she told herself. Both of them were stubborn and hot-tempered.

She smiled helplessly into the bathroom mirror as she prepared for her morning shower. Her eyes were red from lying awake most of the night and faint circles had taken residence just above her high cheekbones.

Surprisingly, breaking off her relationship with Rhonda had left her with little lingering pain. She supposed the time lapse between the betrayal and the present had served as a time of grief and healing.

Now she needed to get on with her life, forgetting Rhonda *and* Hazy.

One thing she was sure of, resolved the previous night as she lay awake in bed, she had to see and talk to Hazy again. She had to make things right between them. She couldn't get on with her life with Hazy's anger hanging over her.

Facing her would require a tremendous amount of courage, more than she felt she could summon, but somehow she would have to do it, would have to draw on every bit of strength she could muster.

And how she looked, her confidence level, would play a big part in this.

Nina dressed carefully in a full chambray skirt and a white lace blouse. Since she was also meeting Martha for lunch she decided to make herself look and feel as upbeat as possible.

She left her hair unbound and down though, because Hazy liked it that way and this served to boost her confidence as well. Thus armed, she left her cottage and made her way to the rental office.

The small building was deserted but the sound of voices drew her to an open window set in the north wall. From her vantage point, Nina could see Mama New and Heather seated at a weathered picnic table on the far side of the dock.

The two were working earnestly, fashioning clothing for several naked dolls lined up side by side on the tabletop. Mama New was wielding the needle while Heather fitted the clothing on the dolls.

"Mama, this one just won't go on Polly," Heather said thoughtfully. "Did you sew it right?"

Mama New retreated with a hurt expression. "See here, little bit, I've been sewin' doll clothes since before you were a thought in someone's head. You try that one on her again. Polly's probably been eatin' too much spaghetti this week."

Nina was about to make her presence known when Heather spoke again.

"Mama? Will your dress look like this one when you and Mema go to the church?" She held up a festive creation of frothy white lace.

"Lord gull, no," Mama New answered with a deep chuckle. "There's no way your Mama could wear something like that. My shape couldna handle anything with all that lace and ruffles. It would make it hard for me to fit through the door of the church, now wouldn't it?"

Heather giggled, but Nina did not wait to hear her response. Silently she left the office and walked to her car.

Chapter 33

"Nina, I just don't understand the change in you," Martha said as she lifted the cherry from atop her mixed drink. "A month ago, you were a bubbly, talkative person. These days you're an out-and-out bore. What *is* the matter?" She delicately devoured the cherry and watched Nina expectantly.

Nina fiddled with the paper napkin beneath her own drink and wondered how best to explain her dilemma to Martha. The two had been close friends for many years and she knew deep inside she could tell Martha anything, yet this thing with Hazy was embarrassing. She found it hard to admit being swept away by such an obvious rogue.

"I don't know if I can talk about it," she finally admitted.

Martha took Nina's slim hand and clasped it between her own.

"Please, Nina, I am your friend. Talk to me, maybe I can help you feel better. Sometimes just talking your problems over can help you put them into proper perspective and even makes solutions more obvious."

Nina did not reply and Martha frowned as if pondering what could be so bad.

"You're not, like, pregnant, are you?" Martha whispered urgently. "I mean, being gay and all…"

Nina smiled, for only the second time that day, and squeezed her friend's hand affectionately. "No, I'm not pregnant. You know better than that."

Martha sat back and sighed. "Well, that's a relief, isn't it? Is it Rhonda? Didn't the two of you get things worked out?"

"Not exactly," Nina began. Then she concluded. "We won't be seeing each other again."

"I thought so," Martha said with a nod. "She asked me to give her a ride over to the shore so she could catch a ride in with her friend, Sean. I thought it was pretty weird she didn't want to wait and leave with me tomorrow."

She paused and examined Nina. "Well, if Rhonda isn't the problem, what is?"

They were dining in the same restaurant they had enjoyed the day before and Nina took a moment to look at the people surrounding them before speaking in a low voice. "I've fallen in love with a woman who's married. Well, not really married but she's going to be soon. She's definitely involved."

Martha leaned forward, as if eager for the intrigue. "Who is it?"

Nina glanced sideways at her friend before answering. "Hazy. You know, the one I'm renting from."

Martha clasped her hands together, suddenly looking much younger than her forty-five years. "I thought there was something going on between you two. I think she's wonderful and she has such a sexy British accent."

Nina shook her head impatiently. "But she's with a woman named Mama New. It doesn't matter about her sexy accent."

"Ahh, I beg to disagree. If she's in love with you then you still have a chance," Martha said with conviction.

"You don't understand. Mama New's husband was killed and he was Hazy's friend, and Hazy's parents were killed in this crash. They...they really need each other. And they have this whole family of children together and there's this one little girl who I suspect is Hazy's by birth because they both have that blond hair and blue eyes. Mama New has darker hair and eyes...I mean, what am I supposed to do? I'm no homewrecker."

Martha leaned back and crossed her long, trouser-clad legs. "I see there's complications, but tell me, what do you want?"

Nina thought carefully for a few moments. "That's the hard thing. A few nights ago, I would have said Hazy, unconditionally, but in the clearer light of day, as they say, I have to reconsider. How could I live with myself if Hazy left Mama New, who is just so precious, for me? I could certainly love helping care for a child like Heather but I could not bear dealing with Mama New's pain. Three parents might be okay in a perfect world but not when there's betrayal and pain involved. I guess now I just want to be alone. I'm thinking I might write a book. Maybe a book about the ocean. Forget all this relationship craziness."

Martha eyed Nina with a skeptical gaze. "I think you are one very confused lady and I'm sorry. I wish I could help but my advice would be to go after Hazy if your feelings are returned. Life's too short, Nina, I've found that out the hard way."

She paused as if in indecision, and then apparently decided to confide in her friend. "I let a dear love get away once and he was later killed in this freak accident while he was working in Germany. I've never quite gotten over it. If I had let myself love and trust him more I might have even had his child so at least a part of him could have lived on."

"Oh, Martha, I didn't know," Nina said, aching with sympathy. She reached and took Martha's hand.

Martha took a large gulp of her drink and nodded. She squeezed Nina's hand and sat back as the waitress brought their plates of food.

"Few people do, Nina," she said after the waitress had left. "But most people have a story like this and that's what I'm trying to tell you. If you really love this woman, work out something. Love is not that easy to find. It's not waiting on every street corner. False love is, but not the real thing."

"So you think I should maybe be her...her mistress or something?" Nina said as she picked at her baked potato.

"I don't know. How do you feel about that?"

"Well, I think the chemistry is certainly there, but no, I don't think it's something I could do. I like Mama New too much and I just, well, I'm not made that way. I couldn't handle the secrecy, and the uncertainty."

"Then I have different advice. Get on with your life but please don't spend it alone. Find someone new to love. It may not be as wonderful but you can find satisfaction. I did."

Nina nodded her agreement as she chewed absently on a piece of shrimp. "Yeah, maybe you're right." She paused. "Are you and Arnie close?" she finally asked. "Do you spend a lot of time together?"

Martha shook her head. "We spend very little time together, actually. He's always off with his computers and I'm always busy keeping the company afloat. You know—" A smile of realization lit her features. "We really don't see one another much, at all. Perhaps that's why we have such a good relationship. The time we do have together is sacred."

Nina laughed, feeling marginally better. "That could be, Martha, that could be." She focused on her dinner.

"I hope I can be best friends with whoever I'm with," she continued after a few minutes. "Since Rhonda was such a jerk, it's given me ample opportunity to re-evaluate what I want in a relationship. I suppose it was a good thing it happened."

Martha stopped with a forkful of food halfway to her mouth and eyed Nina in surprise. "You mean her walking out on you?"

"Yes, I think it will be good for both of us in the long run. Besides, I remembered the other day how angry I always made her just by doing simple things that meant nothing in the grand scheme of things. I would have been on pins and needles the whole time we were together."

Martha nodded her understanding, but pointed an accusing fork at Nina. "You're right. You should have realized that sooner. That's no way to live with someone. But what are you going to do about this Hazy thing? Does she know how you feel? Have you talked to her about it?"

Nina shook her head sadly. "No, but I need to. I went by to talk to her this morning but she wasn't there. Mama New and Heather were there though, and they were talking about what they'll wear when Mama New and Hazy make vows to one another in a church. I couldn't bear it and just had to leave."

"Ouch!" Martha replied. She looked at Nina and sighed.

Chapter 34

Much later that evening, Nina sat at her kitchen table working on the latest novel review.

Darkness had fallen and her world had gotten strangely quiet, as if the whole circle of rental cottages had become deserted. So spying a flash of white startled her and she leaned into the screened window for a closer look.

When her eyes finally adjusted to the gloom outside, Nina saw that Hazy had come onto the boat rental dock, across the drive from her cottage. She was wearing a white T-shirt that periodically caught the lighthouse gleam.

Listening intently, Nina heard Hazy's strong voice carrying a lilting song in another tongue. She listened, trying to discern the words or even the language but it was impossible from this distance.

Nina watched Hazy a long time, aware that she should go out and talk to her but stalling. It was so easy to watch her from a safe distance. Going out and talking to her meant—well, who knew what would happen then?

The singing broke off abruptly and Nina lurched in alarm as Hazy's feet slid from under her and she fell from the upper deck onto the lower one. After a few moments, in which she didn't reappear, Nina slammed her computer closed and raced from the cottage.

Hazy was lying in the shallow level of seawater that covered the boat dock. At first Nina thought she was unconscious, but as she jumped down to rouse her, she heard the slurred refrain of a song and realized she was drunk.

Rethinking her rescue attempt, Nina turned to leave. It would serve her right if she stayed out here all night and caught a chill. But what if she turned face downward and drowned? How high would the tide go? Would it cover her face?

Reluctantly, she grabbed Hazy under the arms and heaved her limp form to the side. Worry beset her as she wondered how she was going to lift her onto the higher deck; the muscular woman was easily twice her own body weight. Hazy saved the situation by rallying and pulling away from her. "Let me be, harridan," she said, her voice slurring. "Don't bother pretendin' what you dona feel."

"Hazy," Nina said coldly, "you've got to get up. You're sitting in water, you know."

Hazy turned her shadowed face Nina's way and her voice reeked of sarcasm. "Of course I know I'm sittin' in water. Do you think I'm an idiot? Oh, s'cuse me, of course you do, otherwise you wouldna have pranced around in your little shirts and panties, breaking the heart of an honest, hardworking—"

"Hazy," Nina pointed out petulantly, "you're not making sense. Just get out of the water so I can go to bed."

She grabbed Nina's forearm so hard that pain shot through to her shoulder. "Yes, go to bed, pretty Nina, I'm sure your Miss Charming waits there f'you. Hey," she added. "Instead of you payin' me, I should've paid you. It was a nice roll in the hay, too,

161

worth a good price."

Nina was so angry her body felt numb. Shaking off Hazy's hand, she leaned and put the weight of her entire body into a forceful shove to Hazy's chest. The strength of the push knocked the taller woman backward, causing a great splash of water as she fell onto the lower planking.

"Drown, damn you, see if I care!" Nina cried.

She moved rapidly toward the safety of her cottage.

Hazy was fast on her heels, amazing Nina with her speed considering the state of her inebriation.

Nina tried to slam the door shut but she was too close behind and threw her body against the door.

"Damn it, get away," Nina growled as she strained to close the barrier.

"Nay, I'll be in, this is *my* place and I'll do as I blasted well please," she replied through clenched teeth.

With a sudden burst of strength, Hazy managed to pop the door from Nina's hands and Hazy, Nina and the door all flew into the room with a mighty crash.

Nina was the first to gain her feet and she stood before Hazy, chest heaving and fists clenched. Breath rasped through her lungs.

"Damn you, Hazel Duncan. I wish I'd never set eyes on you and your blasted cottages!" she shouted.

"Aye, a sentimen' I agree with," Hazy replied weakly. "You've messed up my life enough. Go on back to the..."

Nina watched Hazy, who was sitting on the floor, weave back and forth. She was poised and ready to flee should Hazy renew the attack. But the exertion of chasing Nina had taken its toll. Hazy fell backward onto the carpeted floor and promptly passed out.

Trying to regulate her thudding heartbeat, Nina examined the damage while keeping one eye on Hazy, just in case she was pretending to be unconscious.

The door was mostly whole but the hinge ends of the facing

were splintered and would probably need replacing. Muttering to herself Nina set about straightening as much of the mess as she could.

As Hazy continued to lay insensate, Nina's anger and boldness increased. She passed closer to the supine form, even roughly pulling parts of the doorknob assembly from under her limp body. The memory of Hazy's asinine behavior led her to place a swift kick to the woman's thigh. Though she jumped back nervously, remorsefully, afterward, Hazy still didn't move.

After locking the screen door and leaning the main door against the portal to keep out some of the night air, Nina retreated to her bedroom and crawled into the bed.

Angry thoughts plagued her for many hours and she suddenly realized what she needed to do. Thus resolved, she was able to drift into an uneasy sleep, very aware of Hazy's presence in the next room.

Chapter 35

Hazy woke feeling as though her body had been hit repeatedly with a sledgehammer.

Her mouth was bone-dry. Smacking uncooperative lips and trying futilely to wet them with a dry tongue, she opened her eyes. The first thing she saw was an unfamiliar ceiling. The second thing she saw was Nina's angry face above her.

"I said get up," Nina repeated loudly as she nudged Hazy's ribs with the toe of her sneaker. "If you think I'm going to let you lie around on my floor all day, you are sadly mistaken."

Hazy squinted at her as she tried to make sense of her predicament. "Where am I?" she asked finally, her voice a harsh whisper.

Nina had moved into the bedroom and her voice was muffled. "Guess. By the way, just for the record, you were pretty obnoxious last night."

Hazy sat up, a movement that caused her head to pound

unbearably. "What did I do?" she whispered.

Nina entered the living room, fully dressed and holding a cup of coffee. "Aren't you gone yet?" she asked in a scathing tone. "I have things to do."

Anger sparked in Hazy and she was actually grateful when an outboard motor coughed to life outside the cottage, reminding her of her duties. She wasn't sure what to say to Nina and thought it better if she simply left.

Slowly she rose to prop herself on unsteady legs. Her head began pounding anew and her body felt sorely bruised and battered. A small moan escaped her but sheer willpower helped her hobble to the door.

She turned and looked sadly at Nina when she spied the broken door. "I didn't hurt you, did I?"

Nina stood at the kitchen counter, her back to Hazy. Upon hearing the question, her back stiffened. "No, just a little bruised."

Hazy nodded sagely. Making sure she was not observed, she left the cottage.

Nina released the breath she had been holding. She felt sorry for Hazy but could not let it show. She had to be the strong one, making certain both their lives weren't destroyed by this infatuation.

Wearily she walked into the bedroom and pulled her suitcase and overnight bags from the closet. Most of her clothing was already stacked atop the bed and she mechanically loaded the items neatly into the suitcase. She fetched her toiletries from the bathroom and a few odds and ends she had stacked on one of the bureaus.

Packed last was her work; the Shaner manuscript, the computer and the notebooks she worked in. These were stacked neatly in a canvas bag.

With great sadness, Nina took a few moments to study every familiar corner of the small cottage. She would miss being here. She would miss Hazy and the possibility of who they might have

165

been together.

Hazy had sat at that kitchen table when she conversed with Martha and Rhonda. She'd been waiting on that side of the sofa when Nina returned from the visit with Mrs. Loreli.

And it was on that bed they first made love.

Closing her eyes from the pain stirred by the powerful memories, Nina stood in the center of the living room. Tears broke free and cascaded over her cheeks. Swiping angrily at her face, she grabbed her emotions with a strong mental hand and lifted her handbag from the kitchen table.

She left an envelope with Hazy's name on it in the center of the table. It held the money she owed for the week's rental, the money Hazy had so angrily refused when Rhonda was here.

After pushing the broken door wider so her luggage could get through, Nina left as she had arrived. She knew she was much changed. She would never be that happy, carefree person again.

Chapter 36

After several cups of strong coffee, a light breakfast, and a hot shower, Hazy stood on the wide landing of the dock and stared out across Assateague Channel.

A strong sea breeze ruffled her hair and she made a mental note to get a haircut sometime soon. As always, her eyes were drawn to cottage number eight. This time the sight of the leering door made her wince and shame flooded her. How could she have done something like that? She was often angry but violence had never been a part of her nature.

She couldn't remember all the events of the previous evening but she knew she and Nina had shouted at one another and ended up in actual combat. Hence the broken door.

She sincerely hoped Nina had not been hurt. Her own temper could be fierce but she had yet to hurt a woman physically.

The cottage was very still and Hazy noted that Nina's car was gone. A sense of loss filled her and she wondered how she was going to continue life without Nina when the woman moved into her grandfather's house.

How quickly Nina had entered her life and snared her love. In a mere two weeks Hazy had realized the depth of emotion possible to her, and now she had lost the only person who seemed capable of making her feel those emotions.

Thoughtfully, she watched a small flock of ducks wind their way across the channel toward Assateague. It was almost September. Winter was just around the corner.

Dumping the last of her coffee over the railing into the rollicking seawater, Hazy knew the autumn of her life was also just around the corner. And she had been mostly alone for almost twenty years, never sharing or receiving in more than the most superficial of ways. It was time she grew up and went after the things that made life worth living. And those things included Nina.

Rhonda be damned, Mander be damned. Mama New be damned. Nina was hers to love. And as soon as Nina returned, she would tell her so.

Many hours later, when Hazy was sitting down to a meal prepared by Mama New and Heather, there was a knock on the door of the cottage. Heather ran to answer it, her pink shorts billowing as she raced across the room. Hazy followed at a much slower pace and was surprised to see Mander Sheridan standing there bantering gaily with Heather.

"Hello, Mander," Hazy said guardedly. "What can I do for you?"

"Do you know where Nina Christie is?" Mander asked. "I came to tell her the house is ready for her to start moving in but she's not there. The door's broken too. Do you think she's all right?"

Hazy felt her color rise but answered quickly. "I saw her this morning and she seemed okay. I figured she was out at the house with you."

"No, she never came by," Mander said, running her hands

through her hair in a worried gesture. "What about that door though? Suppose someone took her or something?"

"No, I broke the door myself by accident. I'm waitin' on Manny to bring my toolbox back so I can have a go at fixin' it. I wonder where she is though, no kiddin'." She frowned as several possibilities entered her mind.

"Well," Mander sighed. "I'll be going then. Just tell her the house is ready whenever you see her. I left my key in the pantry." She smiled boastfully and leaned close to Hazy. "I've gotta go— hot date tonight with Ally Charling. She's such a babe."

"But I thought you and Nina...I guess she chose the other one." Hazy said, mostly to herself.

Mander shrugged. "I don't know. I guess we just never hit it off. Not for lack of trying on my part, though. Maybe it's for the best. Ally's a local, easier to get on with."

Hazy stood thoughtfully while Heather told Mander about the latest mishap on her tricycle.

Mama New came forward then and greeted the guest. "Hello Amanda, how've you been, dear?" she said politely. "How's your mother?"

"Oh, she's fine," replied Mander. "Although her headaches are back. Doc Townsend says it's the high blood pressure medication she's taking."

"Well, he's going to change it, isn't he?" Her tone was indignant.

Mander frowned and sighed. "I suppose so, but she's been on this pill about eight years. It'll be tough switching her to something else."

"Tell her I'll stop by and see her next Wednesday when I'm in town."

She paused and swept her heavy arm toward the bar laden with a steaming pot of shrimp, hot corn on the cob and fresh hush puppies. "You'd best come on an' join us for a bite."

Mander looked as though her mouth was watering but she declined the invitation protesting she had to eat with her date. Mama New would not let her leave without a handful of hush puppies, however, and she left happily munching on their steaming, oniony goodness.

"Oh, by the way," she told Hazy through a mouthful of fried bread. "You may want to prop that door a little better. It looks like it might fall any minute. A gust come along and it'll be firewood."

With a wave and a muffled mutter of gratitude for the food, she was gone.

Hazy returned to the bar but the meal was suddenly subdued.

"Mema, what's wrong," Heather said in a piping voice as she smeared her half-ear of corn in the pile of butter she'd heaped on her plate. "You look so sad."

A circle of butter and corn highlighted her lips and Hazy smiled finally as she looked at her. "Nothin', little bit, you just keep workin' on that ear there."

"Hazel," Mama New stated softly. "There's somethin' strange going on here. I think maybe we'd better talk about it."

Hazy studied her dear round face with gentle eyes. "Soon. We'll talk soon."

After dinner, Hazy crossed the Channel Haven driveway toward cottage number eight. Nina still had not returned and Hazy was worried.

Eyeing the broken door she felt shame wash across her again. And to add insult to injury, she probably wouldn't be able to have the door fixed as quickly as she'd hoped.

Perhaps, if Nina didn't mind, she could work on it later this evening or tomorrow. It might also give her a chance to talk with her about the two of them. A swatch of white on the kitchen table caught her eye and she crossed to pick it up. It was an envelope and had her name written across the front.

Suddenly afraid, Hazy held it in her hands for several moments as she gathered courage, one index finger tracing the letters Nina had penned. Upon opening it, her heart painfully skipped a beat.

The envelope held only money. No note, no explanation.

Only money; enough to pay the week's rental. The money said a lot to her. It said Nina was breaking all ties with her, that she was gone and would have no reason to see Hazy again. The envelope full of money said their business contract was complete.

Hazy hung her head as the gloom of evening descended around her.

Chapter 37

Though Nina thought it was Hazy's shouting that woke her the next morning, it took only a minute or two for her to realize the shouting came from two adolescent boys who were frolicking just outside her window.

The window. She had forgotten to close the curtains completely last night and now a hot ray of sunlight was slanting across her face, making her body feel heated and sensual. She longed suddenly for someone—for Hazy—to share the sensation but forced the traitorous thought aside.

Slowly she rose to a sitting position and allowed the coverlet to slide off her satin-clad body. Blinking sleep from her eyes, she peered toward the bathroom of the small cottage she had rented from Mrs. Loreli the day before. Even willing herself in the right direction seemed like too much trouble, and Nina let herself relax back onto the bed.

She had just pulled the coverlet back snugly to her neck when the soft accented voice, which so often haunted her dreams, sounded from within the confines of the room.

"I often feel that way meself, first thing in the morning," Hazy said quietly.

Nina sprang back to a sitting position and studied the room. Try as she might, she couldn't see the rogue.

"I'm here in the chair by the door," she said with a soft sigh.

"How dare you," Nina said, the words barely audible in the now quiet morning air. "How dare you enter my room while I'm sleeping? I've never met anyone as rude as you."

"It's okay, love, I meant no harm. I was actually enjoying watching you sleep. Angelic you are, then. Quite different from when your eyes are open."

Wrapping the coverlet around herself, Nina swung her feet to the floor. "I can't believe you've broken into one of Mrs. Loreli's cottages. I hope she strings you up."

She paused and uncertainly eyed the dark corner where the voice hailed from. "I didn't leave the door unlocked, did I?"

"No," Hazy assured her. "I unlocked it and came in."

"Unlocked it? I don't understand. Mrs. Loreli would never have given you the key to my room."

Hazy sighed and leaned forward. Now Nina could glimpse the lightness of her hair amid the gloom of the corner. "Emma had no choice. I'm a working woman, Nina," Hazy said, her voice very low and very soft. "And I choose to make my living off the tourist trade. I have several places here on the island, and I'd hoped to find you at one of them. I've been checking registers most of the morning. And here you are."

"If that isn't the most low-down, underhanded thing I've ever heard," Nina ground out. "Just because you own a couple rental businesses does not give you the right to go barging into people's private rooms. That's what we pay our rent for, you pompous ass. This cottage belongs to me as long as I pay my rent and you have no right coming in here. Now leave!"

"Nina, you don't understand. I had to see you. This is our last chance to be together. You don't need Rhonda or anybody else. You and I belong together, can't you see that?"

"Yes, I see," Nina replied hotly. "I see what you're trying to do." She paused for breath. "What are you planning to do with me, Hazy? Set me up in some nice little apartment somewhere and come see me when the urge hits you?"

Hazy looked puzzled by her words. "Nina, why do you need an apartment? You have a house already."

"You are such an idiot!" she shouted as she came to her feet beside the bed. "As if something like that would go on in Grandpapa's house! Just get out of here and leave me alone. I can't stand to be in the same room with you. You make me sick."

"Surely you don't mean that, ducks," Hazy replied softly. "Look, let's pack your things and we'll go back to Channel Haven and work this all out. We've got all the time in the world to clear up these misunderstandings."

She moved to stand close to Nina. "Please?"

Nina was much too aware of her nearness and her own partial state of undress even to think coherently. She inhaled Hazy's delicious scent and felt the air around her grow warm with body heat as Hazy approached. Feeling herself becoming lost in the sensation of Hazy's nearness, she reacted to save herself in the only way she knew how. Brutally.

"Go away, Hazy. Do you really believe I could want you? I... have everything now. Rhonda is very rich."

Her throat choked on the words as she tried to convince herself it was only an implied lie, not a direct one.

Hazy reacted as she'd hoped. She pulled away with a shocked hiss and her anger laddered until it fairly crackled against the walls of the room. It was several more moments before she found her voice but her breathing sounded loud and harsh in the small room.

"All right then," she said in a voice as cool as Antarctic wind. "Have it your way. Goodbye, Nina."

Hazy walked from the room, slamming the door behind her.

A sudden sense of loss left Nina with weak knees. She wanted to run after her, call her back but felt her legs would not support her weight if she tried to move. She sank back onto the bed and the gulls outside picked up her pitiful weeping and carried the cries, echoing them, to the sky.

Chapter 38

When Nina's parents found her later that afternoon, she was sitting on top of a sand dune which bordered Little Oyster Bay.

She had been crying off and on for most of the morning and had a blistering headache. The sibilant water of the bay had not helped her mood as she'd hoped, so she had spent the past hour or so wondering where to go and what to do to take her mind off her loss.

She viewed the arrival of her parents as a blessing and a curse. They would distract her, true, but they might also see through her crocodile smiles to the pain underneath. She didn't relish the idea of explanations, especially to her parents.

"We were worried about you," said her father as he approached Nina and pulled her to her feet. "I actually thought you might have run away because Rhonda showed up again."

Her mother stood on his right; a frowning Mrs. Loreli on his left. Nina studied her parents, noting anew what a handsome, happy couple they were. Her father's tall athletic body always hovered protectively over her mother's small form and her mother seemed to relish that comfort. Freda's perfectly coiffed hair was almost solid white now and Nina had a hard time remembering the exact shade of auburn it had been. Throughout Nina's youth it had been worn braided and wound into a neat coil atop her head. Then, three years ago, she'd had it styled short and rinsed to highlight the white. Nina thought it a lovely improvement, the cut framing her mother's face and striking green eyes perfectly.

Nina smiled bravely and patted her father's arm to reassure him. "No, we just talked and decided we had nothing in common anymore."

Patrick Christie grinned. "Hey, I could have told you that if you'd have asked me. I never thought she was the right one for you."

"Paddy, hush!" said Nina's mother, "leave the girl be." Turning to Nina, she embraced her daughter then studied the tear-stained face. "How are you, Nina, are you all right?"

Nina wanted very badly to cry in her mother's arms as she had when she was a little girl, but this was her problem now and Mommy's arms couldn't take away the pain as they once had.

"I'm fine. Just enjoying the bay. Isn't it pretty?"

Her mother's sigh indicated she would go along with Nina's ploy to change the subject. "Yes, I've always loved it here. I wish I could have spent more of my island years here rather than always over on the channel."

"You know, I wish we'd bought property here ten years ago," said Patrick in a musing tone, "we could have increased our investment tenfold by now."

Nina and her mother's eyes met and they rolled them heavenward simultaneously.

Patrick watched them, enjoying the old game. "What? What did I say?"

As if suddenly remembering Mrs. Loreli, Freda turned and pulled the woman close. "Emma wants us all to take a swim with her. What do you think?"

Nina was silent a moment then reminded herself that life had to continue. "Sure," she sighed finally. "Sounds like fun."

"I told them they could use your cottage to change into their suits, is that okay?" Mrs. Loreli asked Nina. "The girls are readying a room for them, but it's going to take a while."

Nina nodded but eyed Mrs. Loreli suspiciously, wondering why she hadn't told Nina that she didn't actually own Sweeping Pines. Did she simply manage the cottages for Hazy? Nina remembered her harsh words about Hazy during their earlier conversation and wondered how much of that was due to sour grapes over being bought out by the businesswoman. She remained silent, however, walking and dusting sand off her shorts at the same time. She led the way to her cottage and ushered her parents inside.

Later, swimsuits dripping, Nina and her mother sat on the dock and watched as Emma coached Patrick on the fine art of sailboarding. Try as he might, Nina's father couldn't master the skill of balancing atop the board while guiding it through the water. The result was many a hilarious spill and Nina and her mother were enjoying the display.

Freda turned to her daughter finally and, placing her sunglasses on her head, studied her intently. "Something's different," she stated firmly.

Nina sighed and reclined back onto the dock, her forearm shading her eyes from the intense sun. Aspirin had eased her headache somewhat. "What do you mean, Mom? What's different?"

"Well, where do you want me to begin," Freda said indignantly. "You're pale, quiet, withdrawn and your eyes have this pained expression they've never had before. Is that enough or do you want more?"

"No," Nina laughed hollowly. "That's enough."

"Well, it's good to hear you laugh, I guess. Is it Rhonda?"

"No," Nina replied. "I told you it's over. We even separated on decent terms. I was surprised."

"What made the two of you split up? What caused what she did to you, running off that way?"

Nina shrugged, bored with the topic. "I don't know. Cold feet on her part. Overall, she just doesn't appeal to me anymore."

"So…" Freda eyed her daughter sideways, as if gauging her reaction to her next question. "Is there someone else?"

"No, and I hope there won't be for a very long time."

Freda fell silent but Nina could sense her dismay. Warm ocean breezes frolicked across their skin and Nina focused on that.

Patrick joined them a short time later, scattering water droplets and making the two women squeal. He was slightly out of breath from his climb up the sea oats-covered bank and huffed beside them a moment or two before speaking.

"Hey, Emma wants us to eat dinner with her at The Shallows this evening. What do you girls say?"

"I think it's a wonderful idea," cooed Freda. "What about you, Nina?"

"Yes, that sounds nice," she replied mechanically, pasting on a bright smile. "I've always wanted to see what the inside of that club looked like, and now I'll get the chance."

"It's not that big a deal," said Freda. "I went there with Papa a few times."

"Grandpapa Tom belonged to The Shallows?" Nina hadn't realized her grandfather had belonged to the island's only version of a private club.

"Oh sure, all the old-timers were members," said Patrick, his fingers combing water from his graying hair.

Freda grimaced at him. "Old-timers? What a thing to say!"

She turned back to Nina. "What he means to say is the club was established by the old fishing families to provide some activities apart from the fishing seasons and later, from the influx of tourists each year. The members are mostly long-term locals plus a few newer imports who live here full time. Like you, honey, maybe you should apply for membership."

Nina nodded thoughtfully. "Maybe I will. I met some really nice locals last week. Do you know Cyrus Leppard?"

"Oh, my gosh," Freda exclaimed. "Do I know Uncle Cyrus? He was the one who took me out for an ice cream cone and a tour of the bay on the *Lady Say* when my mother died so suddenly. I was glad because I didn't have to be with Papa right then." Her eyes had taken on the sheen of memory recalled. "I sure do know him and there never was a sweeter man alive than old Uncle Cyrus."

"Hey," Patrick interjected playfully. "What about your dear husband?"

Freda leaned and kissed him quickly on the lips. "Now honey, you know you are the very sweetest."

"Umm hmm," he grunted, feigning indignation.

"Tell me all about him, Nina. How did he look? What was he doing?" Freda demanded.

Freda's animation was infectious and soon Nina was sharing with her all the latest news of the island.

Patrick, easily bored, soon lumbered down the embankment to give sailboarding another try.

Chapter 39

As soon as the sun lowered in the west, the Christie family and Mrs. Loreli returned to Sweeping Pines. Nina's parents set about securing a cottage for themselves and they separated to dress for dinner.

After a shower, Nina began to feel better about her situation with Hazy. She still harbored worlds of hurt and anger toward her, but knew it would fade if given time. The old adage, time heals all wounds, was very true. And, healing would be helped along even more if she stayed away from the woman. She wondered if Hazy would ever forget Nina's harsh last words.

Due to a lack of choices, Nina was forced to wear the same blue dress she'd worn the night of Aaron Clark's houseboat party. She dressed it up with pearls and diamonds, and swept her long hair into a painstaking French braid clasped with a pearl barrette, a gift from a great-aunt on her father's side.

She took a good bit of time on her makeup as well, applying

cosmetics to enhance her eyes and bring out her high cheekbones. White leather pumps completed her ensemble. Fetching up a white lace shawl, she pulled it across her shoulders and then walked across the grassy expanse that separated her cottage from her parents'.

Freda looked ravishing in a dress of red watered silk that brought radiance to her short white hair and darkly tanned skin. She was a thin woman of small stature, and the red dress's elongated style made her appear taller and emphasized every curve. High black leather heels added to the effect, and her neck and ears sparkled with diamonds every time she moved.

Patrick was dressed as usual, his tall, stocky body encased in a tailored business suit, but for this special occasion he'd chosen a red silk tie that matched his wife's dress. His gray hair was neatly styled and he smelled pleasantly of patchouli cologne.

"I can't believe my good fortune," Patrick said as he and Freda came from their cottage. "I get to escort two of the loveliest ladies on the island to dinner."

"Make that three," said Freda with a smile as she inclined her head toward the parking area. Nina and her father turned and saw Mrs. Loreli coming toward them.

Nina had never seen her look as lovely. She wore a gauze dress printed with a small floral pattern. Her long steel gray hair was pulled into a neat bun, but wisps of curly hair had escaped and framed her smiling, friendly face. As a final touch, she wore flat, soft ballet shoes and carried a small black handbag.

"Well, aren't we a troupe," she teased as she got close. "I am so looking forward to this. I seldom get the chance to dress up and go out to dinner, so this is a special treat."

Taking the scenic route to the restaurant, riding in the Christie's air-conditioned sedan, they drove south along Deep Hole Road and along Maddox Boulevard to Main Street.

The Shallows club was located in a small isolated pocket of land near Chincoteague High School. From her father, Nina learned that The Shallows started life in 1901 as an all-male, all-local "smoking" club, where men could go to escape their wives' genteel ways. By the Fifties women had been grudgingly included in the membership and all the members banded together to draw up a new charter to keep the membership confined to local fishermen's families. A rough pool was installed with tennis courts coming later and soon the children of the local families made up much of the club's clientele. When the main club building blew down in the great storm of 1966, these same children helped rebuild and, later, when they were grown, add on to the main house. The club had remained pretty much the same since that time, still locally owned and exclusive in its membership. Mrs. Loreli had to show her membership card before they were allowed through the tall wooden-post gates, even though everyone at the gate greeted her by name.

The lovely landscaped grounds and the Victorian-style house that held the conjoined restaurant and tavern impressed Nina. The interior of the house featured tasteful memorabilia from the fishing industry's heyday. Most of the occupants of the restaurant were middle-aged and lounged casually at white-clothed round tables.

A pleasantly plump, soft-spoken woman greeted them and escorted them to a corner table lit by candlelight. A server immediately brought them tumblers of iced water.

Nina smiled gratefully to her father as he held her chair for her and she clasped her mother's hand, some of her old fire returning in these elegant, relaxed surroundings. Behind her, a quartet of classical musicians began a lilting melody.

While they waited for their drinks, Patrick took Mrs. Loreli's hand and drew her onto the dance floor. They swayed expertly together, even though Mrs. Loreli's years greatly outpaced her father's. Nina and Freda watched, even laughing and clapping softly at an especially difficult step.

The evening progressed well and after sating themselves on excellent food and wine, Patrick asked his daughter for a dance. Thrilled, Nina followed him onto the floor, swept into his secure embrace. He spun her through a waltz as he commented humorously on every aspect of island life. Nina found his silliness relaxing and familiar and smiled at his antics. And it was in the middle of a laugh when she spied a familiar form across the dance floor.

She stilled immediately and searched hard through the restaurant's dimness. Was it Hazy? It was hard to tell because every time she spied the person, her companion, another tall blond woman, blocked Nina's view.

Several moments later, she caught a glimpse of a too-familiar face. It *was* Hazy Duncan.

Chapter 40

She was sitting with another of her conquests, a tall, elegant woman who had matching platinum hair. The new girlfriend was dressed in a simple green dress and it was obvious to Nina that simple was her way; she was so beautiful that she needed no decoration.

They were laughing together and Nina was angered by Hazy's apparent happiness and nonchalance when she herself felt so badly.

Looking up, Hazy caught her eye and Nina found satisfaction in the shock that registered on her face. The shock was soon replaced by cool animosity and she studiedly turned her face away.

"Nina? What's wrong?" her father said next to her ear. "I didn't step on your toe, did I?"

She leaned back and smiled up at him. "Of course not. I just thought of something I need to do later."

Like knock Hazy's head off, she finished to herself. How could she be out with another woman so quickly after professing to care for her so much?

She had half a mind to seek out Mama New and show her evidence of this scoundrel's infidelity. Rational thought intruded; she too was guilty in this scenario of infidelity.

She was also out dancing. Still, she was with her family and it galled her to think that after Nina's rejection of her, Hazy had immediately arranged something with another woman. The bitch!

She craned her neck slightly, trying to get another glimpse of her. Imagine having dinner together out in the public eye! How many times had people warned her about the smallness of the island and how everyone knew everyone else's business? Hazy was deliberately hurting Mama New by her careless actions. Nina chewed her bottom lip, frustration and hurt filling her completely.

The music ended and she and her father returned to their table. Patrick was watching his daughter closely, as if sensing that something was wrong. Nina tried not to see as he exchanged a puzzled glance with her mother. He bent to his peach cobbler, delivered to their table as they danced.

Nina took a deep sip of water and tried to avoid looking at Hazy's table. She could feel those bright blue eyes on her though, and she fancied the gaze burned as it touched her bare skin. Unavoidably her eyes were compelled to study Hazy again.

She looked so beautiful this evening. Wearing a short white jacket, tailored to hug her broad shoulders and tight waist, she had countered it with loose trousers of pale linen and a cobalt blue shirt, low cut and rounded at the neck. The shirt was tight and hugged her perfect body closely. Simple but elegant.

She finally realized what was so very different about her appearance; she had pulled her shaggy hair into two decorative combs along the sides of her head, which gave her a very different appearance. The style highlighted her sharp cheekbones and gave her face a more severe, mature air.

Nina imagined she could smell her scent and a strange tingling sensation overtook her body.

Quickly she surveyed her own table. Had anybody noticed? No one was looking at her, so she continued her observation.

Hazy was talking animatedly to the blond woman and Nina's mind drifted as she watched. Her thoughts flew back to the night they'd shared, when Hazy's touch had been like a brand marking her skin. It was amazing the heat of this one woman. Perhaps her many hours in the hot sun stockpiled the sun's energy and she only let it escape after the sun left for the night. She smiled dreamily at the thought. Hazel, the solar storage unit.

Moments later Nina sensed a different type of heat and realized Hazy was eyeing her angrily. She was mortified. She'd caught Nina watching her, caught her mooning like any stupid schoolgirl. Nina tucked her head and saw Mrs. Loreli regarding her closely. It was all a bit too much.

Standing suddenly, Nina excused herself and walked purposefully toward the ladies' room, praying neither her mother nor Mrs. Loreli would follow. She ran cold water in one of the basins and gingerly patted her face and neck with it.

She definitely needed to cool her ardor. How many more times was she going to make a fool of herself over this ogre of a woman? Hazy must be having a jolly laugh telling her girlfriend about the stupid woman who took her into bed, then rejected her persistent advances outright, and later mooned over her in public places. No, how ridiculous. She would never warn this new victim of her own impending fate.

She felt like such an idiot. Clasping a paper towel to her face, she blamed Hazy. If she didn't possess such magnetism, Nina wouldn't be in this predicament.

She studied her reflection in the mirror with jaded eyes. Every time she was near Hazy, she felt as though she were moving through a sensual fog, a fog that made her oblivious to everything around her except Hazy.

Probably the same thing had happened to Mama New several years ago. She probably fell for her when she was married to Newt, unable to help herself. Well, now she was paying the price.

Straightening her clothing and stiffening her spine, Nina checked her appearance one last time in the mirror and opened the door.

A hatefully familiar voice whispered beside her. "Is the ladies' empty?"

Nina turned toward Hazy, in shock. "What did you say?"

"I said," she repeated slowly, one palm pressed firmly against the wall of the hall. "Is it empty?" She nodded toward the ladies' room.

Nina's mouth quivered and she bit her bottom lip. "Yes, it's empty. Go right in."

She turned to return to the dining room but Hazy moved swiftly and grabbed her hard around the waist, propelling her forcibly through the ladies' room door. An image of a shattered cottage door filled her mind so she relaxed slightly and didn't fight, although a muffled shriek of surprise did escape.

Hazy pushed her against the inner wall and propped her left forearm above Nina's head to prevent the outer door from opening.

"Nina, you make me so..." she began angrily. But their lips were mere inches away and she simply leaned forward a bit and took possession of Nina's trembling lips.

At first, Nina resisted, but the nearness overwhelmed her and she found herself lost in the kiss, hypnotized by the slow roving of lips and tongue as Hazy thoroughly kissed her. Soon the two were straining together, fumbling with each other's clothing, blindly uncaring of where they were; only knowing that the need to be unclothed and connected together overrode all caution.

A sudden push against the outer door brought reality back with shattering force.

Nina gasped and clutched her loosened dress to her bosom. Her eyes found Hazy's face and widened at what they had almost done.

Hazy still wore a dreamy expression, slow in returning from the web of passion that had snared her.

"Hazy!" Nina ground out in an urgent whisper as she tried to refasten her dress. "What are we going to do?"

Coming alert suddenly and acting with a speed borne from years of boating, Hazy held the door with one arm and her body while at the same time whirling Nina with her free hand and quickly fastening her clothing.

With shaking fingertips, Nina wiped away her smeared lipstick and tried to fan her crimson cheeks.

"Nina? It's Mother. Are you all right? I thought I heard you cry out."

Nina whirled back to face Hazy and wanted to laugh at the expression on her face. Some of her hair had come unbound and it framed her face, adding to her frustrated, woebegone look.

"Yes Mom, I'll be right there," Nina called. "Wait one minute, please."

Of its own accord, one hand went up to caress Hazy's cheek.

Turning her face, Hazy pressed hot lips into Nina's palm, closing her eyes, seeming to savor the touch. She pulled Nina close and sighed deeply. "Ah Nina, bad timing is our enemy," she breathed against her ear.

"I know, and I'm so sorry we can never be together," Nina whispered back, tears in her eyes.

Hazy pulled away, confused. "Don't say never, love. Meet me tonight, later. We need to work this through."

Nina thought of the blond waiting for her outside and she grew cold. "I need to go, Hazy. And I can't meet you tonight, or any night, okay?"

"Hell no, it's not okay. What do you mean?" Hazy whispered urgently.

"Hazy, I have got to go," she muttered, pulling away.

"Wait." Hazy held her at arm's length and studied her. "You look passable. We can't do anything about your high color, but tell your mum it's from the cold water or somethin'," she told her coolly. "You go first, I'll follow later."

Hazy moved so she'd be behind the door as it opened and Nina left to reassure her worried mother.

Hazy leaned on the vanity and studied herself in the large mirrored wall. Her face bore a defeated expression. It was over. Her body told her differently but her heart knew the truth. Nina had meant what she'd said earlier that morning.

Finally, cloaking her face into a cold mask, she adjusted her clothing, repinned her hair, and moved toward the door.

As she opened the door, a small, elderly woman almost fell through. Hazy caught her and prevented her from falling onto the floor. "Why, Mrs. Harris, do be careful," she chided. "That's a good way to suffer a broken bone, you know."

Mrs. Harris smiled at Hazy and waved one hand nonchalantly. "That's what they give me all those pills for, Hazel, to make my bones strong. I guess I'd bounce like a buoy these days if I fell."

Laughing with difficulty, Hazy left the ladies' room.

Chapter 41

Back at her table, Nina found herself sitting like a corpse throughout the rest of the evening. She saw Hazy return to her table as if she were watching through a glass partition. There was no anger, no sorrow, only numbness.

When the evening was over, Nina bid her parents and Mrs. Loreli goodnight and returned to her cottage.

After sitting for some time, she rose, dropped her dress mechanically onto the chair and fell into bed. Tears found her then and she cried for a love that was lost and also because she knew now that she could never live in Grandpapa Tom's house. This realization broke her heart for she had so looked forward to making the island her home.

There was no way she could remain on the island, not with Hazy here.

How she hated Hazel Duncan for doing this to her!

She knew deep inside that each time she saw Hazy she'd be

reacting the same way as tonight and she just couldn't let that happen.

How could she respect herself, remaining caught up in Hazy's snare of affairs and indiscretions? Poor Mama New. Nina felt only sadness for that kind, sweet woman.

Did all women react to Hazy the same way she did, Nina wondered suddenly. Or was this something unique between her and Hazy?

Angrily, she sat up in the bed and jerked the pearl barrette from her hair. She slung it against the far wall and felt a tug of satisfaction when she heard it break in the darkness.

Then she felt remorse for her actions, thinking of the elderly woman who had given it to her, and cried that much harder. She found it easy to blame Hazy for the broken barrette as well.

She considered going to Hazy's cottage and standing outside, shouting out her indiscretions so everyone in every cottage in that complex could hear. So what if her reputation was ruined? So what if she had to leave the island in disgrace? At least Hazy would be ostracized by the moral islanders and would have to take responsibility for her actions.

Then she thought of her parents, envisioned their shocked, dismayed faces. She saw Mama New's hurt expression in her vivid imagination as well as Heather's bewilderment and she knew she could never do such a thing.

The people here probably already know about her anyway, she consoled herself. Maybe they only pretended to like Hazy.

She thought over her options. Leaving the island would be like losing an old, dear friend. She loved this place, with its harsh winds, glorious sunsets and riotous animal life. Thoughts of the water, of how it changed color according to the season, always made her spirit lighten. And the marsh grass, fading from the bright green of spring to a burnt golden by fall, roots filled with swarming sea life. She had been looking forward to her first full winter here. She remembered them as gloriously intense during holiday visits to Grandpapa Tom.

She thought of grandfather's house, which now would always be called by his name, The Border, in her mind. Grandpapa Tom had wanted her to live there, had wanted her to be a part of the legacy of island love he had left for her. How could she sell his house? How could she leave it empty and falling into decline? There were no easy answers.

Going back to the congestion of the city now would be very hard indeed. Was there any conceivable way she could stay on the island? Could she be hard-hearted enough to ignore Hazy and her entire establishment? She thought of what Hazy had told her in this very room that morning. That she owned several places on the island. What did that mean? Exactly how active was she in island business? Would she run into her often during the course of any given day?

Wearily she punched at her suddenly irritating pillow. All Hazy would have to do was approach her when she was alone and she knew, without a doubt, that she would be in her arms again. The woman had that effect on her, plain and simple.

The thing to do was escape. Leave behind all her hopes and dreams and escape the conniving she-devil who had ruined her life.

Chapter 42

Mama New took a seat in one of the Adirondack chairs on the dock outside the office. Business had been slow that morning so Hazy was not surprised to see she was taking a little break. She was not prepared for the ultimatum, however.

"Hazy, it's time," Mama New said quietly.

Hazy sighed and pulled herself from the railing where she'd spent most of the morning, standing, staring out at the ocean. "Time for what, Carrie?" she asked, even though she knew.

"Hazel, I've known ye all of our lives and I've never seen you this way. I'm frankly insulted that ye're na talking to me, your dearest friend, about what's been goin' on."

Hazy sat in the chair next to her and leaned forward with her forearms on her knees. She clasped her hands together. "I'm sorry, love. I truly am."

"It's her, isn't it? Nina."

Hazy looked over and saw that Mama New's chin was set

firm and it jutted out toward the channel. "It is. I can't begin to tell you what I feel for her."

"I'm not sure I want to know," Mama New said heatedly.

"You don't?" Hazy was surprised.

Mama New turned and faced her square on. Her mouth was grim.

"You're going to treat her just like all the others," she chided. "You're going to break that poor child's heart; break all of our hearts again."

She paused and drew in a deep breath. "Now, you know I love you, always have, but I just canna stan' by and watch while you stomp all over that sweet young girl." Her voice rose. "I tell you I can't take it, Hazel. I won't. I stand firm on that. You need to send her away."

Hazy reached and took Mama New's hands in hers. "No, no, it's not like that. Really." She sighed and squeezed the hands. "I hear what you're saying and God help me. I know it's true. Has been true. This is different, though."

Mama New eyed her doubtfully. "How so?"

"I love her more than life itself, I do," Hazy said with conviction.

Mama New wriggled free and rose to approach the railing. She seemed to be unable to look at Hazy.

Hazy stood and followed her.

"Do ye ken what ye're sayin', Hazel?" Mama New asked quietly. She looked up at Hazy with squinted eyes. "Do ye understand what it means?"

Hazy nodded and hung her head as she replied. "I do, Carrie. I do. And I wanted so badly to share my life with her. Start a whole new life with her. But it'll not be."

"Aye?"

"She'll na have me. She tells me she wants to be with the other girl. The rich one."

"But Hazy, you're…" She broke off, then continued. "Look here, it's for the best then, if that's what she's after, there's no place here for her."

Hazy nodded and bit her bottom lip. "When does the pain go away?"

Mama New pulled Hazy into an embrace and rubbed her back. "We're doing just fine, my sweet gull, just fine. Time is the great healer."

Hazy nodded into Mama New's shoulder, holding her tightly.

"Come, let's have some tea and talk this out. You've mooned to the ocean long enough, now's time to talk to the livin'," she said, drawing Hazy into the office.

By the time she had finished confiding the details of the past two weeks to Mama New, Hazy was as near tears as she'd ever been in her life. She never cried, wouldn't let herself, but lately had discovered it took less and less to move her to tears.

"Turning into an old softie, that's what," she chided herself as she played out the lines on the rental boats.

She felt comfortable with the solutions she and Mama New had come up with. Time, it was all about time, she chanted mentally. She needed time to clear her head and break free of Nina's spell.

Chapter 43

During breakfast with her parents the next morning, Nina told them of her decision not to live in Grandpapa Tom's house.

"Have you lost your mind?" her father demanded angrily.

Her mother seemed very hurt. "Nina, please reconsider. If you don't live here, the house will have to be sold or rented out. I don't want that to happen," Freda said, wringing her napkin anxiously.

"Well, I'll tell you one thing," Patrick said around a mouthful of toast. "If you think you're going to get out of living in Tom's house without telling us why, exactly why, I think you'd better reconsider."

"Nina, I don't understand," Freda resumed. "You were so excited about the house, so happy to be coming to the island to live. Just yesterday! What has happened to that?"

"What I want to know is who's hurt you to make you decide something like this," Patrick added. "Did someone say something to you? Treat you as unwelcome? What?"

Nina shrugged and kept her eyes cast down into her plate. "I just don't think I like the island as much as I thought I would. Everyone makes mistakes."

"Nonsense," Nina's mother said impatiently. "You've loved it here since you were three years old. You're not being truthful with us and I think we deserve to know why."

She felt so dishonest lying to her parents this way. Why couldn't she tell them the truth? They would understand. They were human too. The shame though, the shame of being duped by Hazy kept her silent.

After almost an hour of wheedling, her parents gave up. After all, she was an adult and had the right to live wherever she chose. Freda finally stopped arguing only when Nina assured her she would find a new apartment close to her parents' home in Alexandria.

"You know it's too late to stop the moving trucks, don't you," Nina's father interjected as a final note. "And I was going to pay for the move but now you'll have to and they'll charge you an arm and a leg for moving your things here then back home. Are you absolutely positive about this?"

This was the final straw for Nina. She had been perilously close to tears during the entire exchange but her father's extreme disapproval, so uncharacteristic of their relationship, proved too much for her to bear. Rising to her feet, she rushed from the restaurant and onto the hot pavement outside.

Since she had ridden to the restaurant in her parents' car, Nina found herself forced to walk back to Mrs. Loreli's. She set out immediately, crossing through several alleys and a grassy field to stay on back roads so her parents couldn't catch up with her as quickly. After walking for about ten minutes, Nina came to the Chincoteague Memorial Park and realized she was at the complete opposite end of the island from Sweeping Pines.

Hot and discouraged, she walked a short way into the park and plopped onto a handy rock to consider her options. She could try to hitchhike to the other side of the island but that way she'd be unable to avoid her parents. She could wait here until her parents finally combed the island and found her. Or she could walk backstreets the hour or so it would take to get to Mrs. Loreli's.

Some choices. She blew dejectedly at a piece of hair that had fallen into her face.

"I know you," said a curious voice behind her. "You stayed at Mema's place."

Nina turned and saw Heather studying her.

Just what she needed. Today was not a good day.

"Yes," she sighed, "I once stayed at Channel Haven. Your name is Heather, right?"

Heather twirled a loose piece of her platinum hair that always seemed precariously bound. "What's your name?"

"Nina," she replied, glancing around the park. "Where's your mama, honey?"

"She's at the water."

Silence descended as they regarded one another. Finally, Heather seated herself on a second rock.

"You must be the one my Mema is in love with."

Her heart thudding, Nina stared at the child but found her cherubic face unreadable. "Why do you say that, Heather?"

"I heard her telling Mama all about it," she replied quickly, then, lowering her voice conspiratorially, she confided, "I wasn't s'posed to listen but I have this place where I can hear real good." She paused and squinted at her confidant. "You won't tell, will you?"

"Oh no," Nina hastened to reassure the little girl. "What else did you hear?"

"Oh, lotsa t'ings," Heather said, her voice taking on a boastful quality. "I hear Sammie and Alice fight. They're so stupid I can't stand it."

Nina's mind had drifted and she wasn't really listening anymore. If Hazy had told Mama New that she loved her...No, the quandary still existed. Was this what she wanted? A life with Hazy Duncan at the expense of the others?

"When did Hazy, your Mema, tell your Mama that she loved me?" Nina asked suddenly.

"Just this morning," said Mama New coolly as she approached from Nina's left.

"Well, there you are," she said to her daughter as Nina gaped at her. "I thought I'd lost you."

"Sorry, Mama," the child chimed automatically.

"Well, stay closer next time. Why don't you go swing now, just over there, and let me talk to this lady."

"Okay." The child called to a watching squirrel and blissfully skipped after it.

Mama New settled herself onto the vacated rock and stared out across the channel waters. Several seconds ticked by. The woman seemed to be mulling over what she would say.

"I don't mean to pry, Miss Nina, but for the life of me I can't understand why you feel the need to hurt our Hazy this way." She faced Nina. "Then again, maybe I can understand it. She doesn't always put her best foot forward now, does she?"

"No," Nina choked out in amazement.

She had expected anger, pain, accusations, but here was Mama New calmly asking why Nina was hurting *her* lover.

"Mama New, I—"

"I know, I'm a busybody," Mama New exclaimed, holding up her hands, "but if you can't help the people you love, what's the purpose of bein' on this earth? Answer me that."

"Well," Nina replied, her head spinning from this astounding turn of events. "I suppose you're right."

"Yes, I reckon I am." Mama New's tone softened and she leaned forward, studying Nina's face. "You don't *seem* the type who cares only for the finer things of the world."

She sighed and leaned back. "Hazy has been so good to me, Miss Nina. I know she comes across rough, but she's such a heart inside. Give you the shirt off her back, she will. And so good with Heather too, teachin' her the ways of the island and the sea. She'll be a fine partner if she can find someone to get through the hull she's built around herself. And I believe that's what you did, little miss, you got right through to her in a big way."

Again she held up her hands. "Oh, I saw she'd been acting so strange and I tol' her that she just had ta tell me what ta trouble was. I'd it figured some, but the way she told it fair made tears start to my eyes. She thinks the world of you, Miss Nina, but neither of us can quite figure out exactly why you're runnin' from her. Did you really find someone else? Someone with more money?"

"But Mama New," Nina protested, amazement in her voice. "It's not that. I thought you and Hazy were together, that the two of you were a couple and Heather your child."

Mama New appeared stunned at this revelation. "Hazy and me, that way? Oh, no, love, ye got it all wrong. Hazy and me just taken care of one 'tother. We're like brother and sister."

"But what about Heather? Isn't she Hazy's daughter? She's the image of her," Nina protested.

Mama New stared at her in astonishment. Realization dawned visibly and she chuckled. "Wait a minute," she said with a secretive smile. "This should clear ta up."

Glancing around to make sure they weren't observed too closely, she reached deep into the bodice of her dress and retrieved a small rectangle. Passing it to Nina, she said, "This is my Seth."

Nina took the small object, still warm and fragrant from Mama New's body, and studied it. A man's face stared back at her from a laminated photograph. His face was lined and ruddy from the elements but his wide smile and crinkled, twinkling eyes immediately bespoke a young, fun-loving nature. Atop his head was a shock of the same platinum, white-blond hair that adorned Heather's head. And he could have been Hazy's twin.

"Oh," Nina said dumbly.

"The hair is common among the island folk here. Seth and

Hazel been best friends since grade school," Mama New told Nina softly. "Lots of people thought them brother and sister, they were so much alike."

She chuckled. "And I had to come between their friendship some when Seth and me started courtin' and let me tell you, it was a task with both of them charmin' me off my feet. Or dealing with their devilment, I should say. I loved my Seth, though, and his friends became mine. Hazy, though I love her dearly, ain't much like me. I have no love of books and readin' and such as she does. It's a lonely road she walks."

She turned her face back to the water. "I miss my Seth. And my life was perfect up until he was taken from me." She sighed audibly. "I've often wondered why the good Lord saw fit to take him away but I'm a good Christian woman and won't question it more than a few times."

Nina was stunned. Hazy and Mama New were friends only. Close, like siblings.

Her heart suddenly lurched in delight as the realization hit her. She could have Hazy. She no longer had to fight against the attraction that insistently pulled them together.

"So tell me now, was that the only reason you was puttin' Hazy off," Mama New asked, amusement shining in her dusky eyes.

"Yes," Nina admitted. "I thought she was with you. If you were partners—well, I'd have no part of that. I like and admire you and wouldn't dream of trying to lure her away from you. I felt so helpless. Hazy and I seem to have this attraction, some type of chemistry between us." She grinned sheepishly at the admission. "I have a hard time behaving myself when she's around."

Mama New laughed and slapped one of her hearty thighs. "It was just that way with Seth and myself. Sometimes I felt as though I didn't belong in polite society."

"Do you think Hazy knows the way I feel?" Nina asked.

"Well that's what's got her so bamboozled. She'd been getting hot and cold from you, so never knowed exactly what was going on in that pretty head of yourn," Mama New replied.

"I've got to tell her," Nina said, leaping to her feet. "Is she at Channel Haven?"

Mama New's face suddenly fell what looked to Nina like a half a mile.

"Oh, goodness," Mama New said curtly.

Nina was alarmed. "What's the matter?"

"Hazy is gone."

"What do you mean, gone. Where has she gone?"

Mama New stood abruptly and began moving toward the parking area. "Come on, Nina, maybe we can catch her before she shoves off," she called over her shoulder as she scooped Heather from one of the swings.

In Mama New's very old, but very tidy pickup truck, Heather ensconced between them, they bounced over the rough island back roads as Mama New explained that Hazy had decided the night before to leave for one of her week-long fishing excursions. And this was the reason Mama New and Heather were taking advantage of the park, because they knew they'd be tied down to the business until she returned.

"We've got to catch her," Nina muttered as they gained the quiet village streets. "Hurry, Mama New, I don't think I can wait a whole week to be with her."

The older woman grinned and drove even faster.

Within several minutes they arrived at the same boarding dock on Chincoteague Bay where Aaron Clark lived in his houseboat.

Nina was out of the truck before it even came to a complete stop. She knew which boat was Hazy's and knew exactly where it was berthed.

Chapter 44

Hazy was loading the final box of canned and freeze-dried food onto her thirty-five-foot cruiser, *Shepherd's Moon*, when she heard the voice that had been etched into her heart.

Thinking she was hallucinating, she looked around and her heart leapt in joy when she saw Nina running toward her along the dock. Nina was wearing a long pale blue skirt and a lace blouse and Hazy thought she must be dreaming because she was so beautiful.

But within seconds she was clasped in her arms and they were holding each other close.

"Nina," she said with a sigh. "I almost didna believe you were real."

Nina pulled back and smiled up at her. "Of course I'm real. Are you glad I'm here?"

Hazy laid her hands alongside Nina's face and pressed a firm kiss to her lips. "What do you think? I'm...I don' know what's going on."

Nina spoke rapidly. "Hazy, I thought you and Mama New were together, a couple, and that Heather was your little girl."

Hazy dropped her hands and stepped back to study Nina with a mystified expression. "Wherever did you get that idea? She just lives in the cottage next to mine. What did you..."

Nina shook her head, shrugging her helplessness about the misunderstanding. "Several people referred to her as your better half and, since she was always there..."

"You thought..." A deep chuckle welled in Hazy's chest.

"So that's why I acted kind of..."

Hazy lifted her pale eyebrows. "There's nothin' quite like jumpin' to conclusions, now is there?"

"I beg your pardon," Nina said, bristling with mock indignation.

"Ah, love, don't get your feathers riled. Come, let me smooth them for you." Hazy caressed Nina gently along her neck, feeling the pulse there grow stronger.

"Hazy?"

"Yes, love?" She waited attentively.

"That lady you were with last night...is she...are you and she?"

Hazy laughed aloud, having never felt happier, and spun Nina by one hand as if dancing. It made the blue skirt twirl about her knees.

"One misunderstanding after another," she said. "I'm not much a believer in incest, Nina. That was Beatrice, my youngest sister. I have two sisters here, as I told you. You'll be meetin' them directly, I suppose, but later. I want you all to myself for now." She pulled Nina into her arms and nibbled at an earlobe.

Nina wiggled away from Hazy's arms, strode onto the boarding plank and grabbed her hand to pull her along. "Let's go back to Channel Haven."

Hazy pulled against Nina's hand, stopping her abruptly. "Ah no, I'm goin' fishin'."

Hazy could feel the passion in her gaze and hoped Nina understood. "Come fishin' with me, Nina." It was a gentle command.

Nina thought of her parents, no doubt looking everywhere for her. She thought of the Shaner novel lying unfinished in a canvas bag. She thought of the new house waiting for her to fill it with life. And she knew it could all wait.

Her parents would see that her possessions were moved into the house and Martha would just have to understand. Love like this only comes along once in a lifetime.

"Okay, Hazy," she said brightly, fondness filling her heart. "Let's go fishing."

"That's my girl," Hazy said with pride in her voice. A new child-like exuberance beamed from her as she asked, "Do we need to go pack a case? You'll need more clothes."

Nina's gaze met Hazy's. She stepped back onto *Shepherd's Moon*. "No. I don't think I'll need them," she replied huskily.

Hazy swept Nina into her arms for one more quick kiss then finished stowing the food.

Seldom taking her eyes from Nina, she switched on the cruiser's powerful engine and rushed to stow the board and let the bowline go. Slowly, she expertly maneuvered *Shepherd's Moon* away from the dock and swung her around.

As they puttered past the marina entrance, Nina leaned over the side and called out to Mama New, standing patiently next to her truck.

"My parents are at Sweeping Pines," she shouted through cupped hands. "Tell them I'm staying and ask if they'll move my things."

She waved and Mama New, with a wide grin, nodded her understanding of the message.

Soon Mama New, Heather and the dock were out of sight.

Much later, after the ship was moving along at the pace of an excited heartbeat, Hazy and Nina sat together at the wheel, Nina between Hazy's spread thighs.

"Hazy," Nina said, watching the circling gulls overhead. "You know, you never did finish telling me the duck fable."

"I didn't, now, did I?" she replied, nuzzling Nina's hair.

"Tell me the rest, please?"

She smiled into Nina's hair. "Can you remember where I left off?"

Nina frowned in thought, "I think the duck was building things but he had no need for them himself because he was so unhappy."

"Oh yes," Hazy began thoughtfully. "But then one day after many years had passed and the duck was very old in spirit, a new duck came to town.

"Now this duck was brown in color and very small, but she was great in spirit and she had just enough spirit to give some back to the little dark duck. He began to live again."

Hazy rubbed one palm along Nina's forearm, caressing her gently. Her rich voice purred as she continued.

"Oh, at first he was angry all the time, because he didn't like the way the little duck made him feel. It frightened him. But finally, he realized that the little brown duck was the best thing to ever happen to him. She was able to replace all that the duck had lost in his life. He even had a desire to build for himself again and to build a life with this little duck."

"And," Nina coached when Hazy was silent for many moments. "What happened then?"

Hazy smiled sweetly at her. "I don't know, ducks, ask me again about thirty years from now."

"Oh, Hazy," Nina chided, with a grin of embarrassed revelation.

Nina looked back at lush, green Chincoteague, her home, its houses muddled in the distance, but the green of the land visible to her across a serene expanse of water. She knew then why the Indians who first settled this area called it Chincoteague. It truly was the 'beautiful land across the water.'

Excitement bubbled within. There was so much to do, so many new things to experience. With Hazy by her side, and the sea in her, the life before her would be grand indeed.

Publications from
Bella Books, Inc.
The best in contemporary lesbian fiction

P.O. Box 10543, Tallahassee, FL 32302
Phone: 800-729-4992
www.bellabooks.com

TWO WEEKS IN AUGUST by Nat Burns. Her return to Chincoteague Island is a delight to Nina Christie until she gets her dose of Hazy Duncan's renown ill-humor. She's not going to let it bother her, though...
978-1-59493-173-4 $14.95

MILES TO GO by Amy Dawson Robertson. Rennie Vogel has finally earned a spot at CT3. All too soon she finds herself abandoned behind enemy lines, miles from safety and forced to do the one thing she never has before: trust another woman.
978-1-59493-174-1 $14.95

PHOTOGRAPHS OF CLAUDIA by KG MacGregor. To photographer Leo Wescott models are light and shadow realized on film. Until Claudia.
978-1-59493-168-0 $14.95

SONGS WITHOUT WORDS by Robbi McCoy. Harper Sheridan's runaway niece turns up in the one place least expected and Harper confronts the woman from the summer that has shaped her entire life since.
978-1-59493-166-6 $14.95

YOURS FOR THE ASKING by Kenna White. Lauren Roberts is tired of being the steady, reliable one. When Gaylin Hart blows into her life, she decides to act, only to find once again that her younger sister wants the same woman.
978-1-59493-163-5 $14.95

THE SCORPION by Gerri Hill. Cold cases are what make reporter Marty Edwards tick. When her latest proves to be far from cold, she still doesn't want Detective Kristen Bailey babysitting her, not even when she has to run for her life.
978-1-59493-162-8 $14.95

STEPPING STONE by Karin Kallmaker. Selena Ryan's heart was shredded by an actress, and she swears she will never, ever be involved with one again.
978-1-59493-160-4 $14.95

FAINT PRAISE by Ellen Hart. When a famous TV personality leaps to his death, Jane Lawless agrees to help a friend with inquiries, drawing the attention of a ruthless killer. No. 6 in this award-winning series.
978-1-59493-164-2 $14.95

A SMALL SACRIFICE by Ellen Hart. A harmless reunion of friends is anything but, and Cordelia Thorn calls friend Jane Lawless with a desperate plea for help. Lammy winner for Best Mystery. No. 5 in this award-winning series.
978-1-59493-165-9 $14.95

NO RULES OF ENGAGEMENT by Tracey Richardson. A war zone attraction is of no use to Major Logan Sharp. She can't wait for Jillian Knight to go back to the other side of the world.
978-1-59493-159-8 $14.95

TOASTED by Josie Gordon. Mayhem erupts when a culinary road show stops in tiny Middelburg, and for some reason everyone thinks Lonnie Squires ought to fix it. Follow-up to Lammy mystery winner *Whacked*.
978-1-59493-157-4 $14.95

SEA LEGS by KG MacGregor. Kelly is happy to help Natalie make Didi jealous, sure, it's all pretend. Maybe. Even the captain doesn't know where this comic cruise will end.
978-1-59493-158-1 $14.95

KEILE'S CHANCE by Dillon Watson. A routine day in the park turns into the chance of a lifetime, if Keile Griffen can find the courage to risk it all for a pair of big brown eyes.
978-1-59493-156-7 $14.95

ROOT OF PASSION by Ann Roberts. Grace Owens knows a fake when she sees it, and the potion her best friend promises will fix her love life is a fake. But what if she wishes it weren't?
978-1-59493-155-0 $14.95

COMFORTABLE DISTANCE by Kenna White. Summer on Puget Sound ought to be relaxing for Dana Robbins, but Dr. Jamie Hughes is far too close for comfort.
978-1-59493-152-9 $14.95

DELUSIONAL by Terri Breneman. In her search for a killer, Toni Barston discovers that sometimes everything is exactly the way it seems, and then it gets worse.
978-1-59493-151-2 $14.95

FAMILY AFFAIR by Saxon Bennett. An oops at the gynecologist has Chase Banter finally trying to grow up. She has nine whole months to pull it off.
978-1-59493-150-5 $14.95

SMALL PACKAGES by KG MacGregor. With Lily away from home, Anna Kaklis is alone with her worst nightmare: a toddler. Book Three of the Shaken Series.
978-1-59493-149-9 $14.95

WRONG TURNS by Jackie Calhoun. Callie Callahan's latest wrong turn turns out well. She meets Vicki Brownwell. Sparks would fly if only Meg Klein would leave them alone!
978-1-59493-148-2 $14.95

WARMING TREND by Karin Kallmaker. Everybody was convinced she had committed a shocking academic theft, so Anidyr Bycall ran a long, long way. Going back to her beloved Alaskan home, and the coldness in Eve Cambra's eyes isn't going to be easy.
978-1-59493-146-8 $14.95

Publications from
Bella Books, Inc.
The best in contemporary lesbian fiction

P.O. Box 10543, Tallahassee, FL 32302
Phone: 800-729-4992
www.bellabooks.com

TWO WEEKS IN AUGUST by Nat Burns. Her return to Chincoteague Island is a delight to Nina Christie until she gets her dose of Hazy Duncan's renown ill-humor. She's not going to let it bother her, though...
978-1-59493-173-4 $14.95

MILES TO GO by Amy Dawson Robertson. Rennie Vogel has finally earned a spot at CT3. All too soon she finds herself abandoned behind enemy lines, miles from safety and forced to do the one thing she never has before: trust another woman.
978-1-59493-174-1 $14.95

PHOTOGRAPHS OF CLAUDIA by KG MacGregor. To photographer Leo Wescott models are light and shadow realized on film. Until Claudia.
978-1-59493-168-0 $14.95

SONGS WITHOUT WORDS by Robbi McCoy. Harper Sheridan's runaway niece turns up in the one place least expected and Harper confronts the woman from the summer that has shaped her entire life since.
978-1-59493-166-6 $14.95

YOURS FOR THE ASKING by Kenna White. Lauren Roberts is tired of being the steady, reliable one. When Gaylin Hart blows into her life, she decides to act, only to find once again that her younger sister wants the same woman.
978-1-59493-163-5 $14.95

THE SCORPION by Gerri Hill. Cold cases are what make reporter Marty Edwards tick. When her latest proves to be far from cold, she still doesn't want Detective Kristen Bailey babysitting her, not even when she has to run for her life.
978-1-59493-162-8 $14.95

STEPPING STONE by Karin Kallmaker. Selena Ryan's heart was shredded by an actress, and she swears she will never, ever be involved with one again.
978-1-59493-160-4 $14.95

FAINT PRAISE by Ellen Hart. When a famous TV personality leaps to his death, Jane Lawless agrees to help a friend with inquiries, drawing the attention of a ruthless killer. No. 6 in this award-winning series.
978-1-59493-164-2 $14.95

A SMALL SACRIFICE by Ellen Hart. A harmless reunion of friends is anything but, and Cordelia Thorn calls friend Jane Lawless with a desperate plea for help. Lammy winner for Best Mystery. No. 5 in this award-winning series.
978-1-59493-165-9 $14.95

NO RULES OF ENGAGEMENT by Tracey Richardson. A war zone attraction is of no use to Major Logan Sharp. She can't wait for Jillian Knight to go back to the other side of the world.
978-1-59493-159-8 $14.95

TOASTED by Josie Gordon. Mayhem erupts when a culinary road show stops in tiny Middelburg, and for some reason everyone thinks Lonnie Squires ought to fix it. Follow-up to Lammy mystery winner *Whacked*.
978-1-59493-157-4 $14.95

SEA LEGS by KG MacGregor. Kelly is happy to help Natalie make Didi jealous, sure, it's all pretend. Maybe. Even the captain doesn't know where this comic cruise will end.
978-1-59493-158-1 $14.95

KEILE'S CHANCE by Dillon Watson. A routine day in the park turns into the chance of a lifetime, if Keile Griffen can find the courage to risk it all for a pair of big brown eyes.
978-1-59493-156-7 $14.95

ROOT OF PASSION by Ann Roberts. Grace Owens knows a fake when she sees it, and the potion her best friend promises will fix her love life is a fake. But what if she wishes it weren't?
978-1-59493-155-0 $14.95

COMFORTABLE DISTANCE by Kenna White. Summer on Puget Sound ought to be relaxing for Dana Robbins, but Dr. Jamie Hughes is far too close for comfort.
978-1-59493-152-9 $14.95

DELUSIONAL by Terri Breneman. In her search for a killer, Toni Barston discovers that sometimes everything is exactly the way it seems, and then it gets worse.
978-1-59493-151-2 $14.95

FAMILY AFFAIR by Saxon Bennett. An oops at the gynecologist has Chase Banter finally trying to grow up. She has nine whole months to pull it off.
978-1-59493-150-5 $14.95

SMALL PACKAGES by KG MacGregor. With Lily away from home, Anna Kaklis is alone with her worst nightmare: a toddler. Book Three of the Shaken Series.
978-1-59493-149-9 $14.95

WRONG TURNS by Jackie Calhoun. Callie Callahan's latest wrong turn turns out well. She meets Vicki Brownwell. Sparks would fly if only Meg Klein would leave them alone!
978-1-59493-148-2 $14.95

WARMING TREND by Karin Kallmaker. Everybody was convinced she had committed a shocking academic theft, so Anidyr Bycall ran a long, long way. Going back to her beloved Alaskan home, and the coldness in Eve Cambra's eyes isn't going to be easy.
978-1-59493-146-8 $14.95

Bella Books

The best in contemporary lesbian fiction

P.O. Box 10543, Tallahassee, FL 32302
Phone: 800-729-4992

www.bellabooks.com